Praise for *Super Schnoz and the Gates of Smell*

★ "The writing, stylistically, has enough action and danger to keep it on the right side of parody, as well as a sense of humor that deftly mixes the absurd with gross-out jokes and clever wordplay. Super Schnoz smells like a winner, especially for reluctant readers."—*Kirkus Reviews*

"With a superhero story line, short chapters, and gross-out humor, the book hits a number of reluctant-reader marks... The book is wacky from page one."—*School Library Journal*

"The puns, references, and nose jokes abound, but themes of friendship and determination are also explored."—*Library Media Connection*

Praise for *Super Schnoz and the Invasion of the Snore Snatchers*

"Bountiful in his nose-related wordplay, Urey crafts fast-moving chapters full of gross-out humor that will surely appeal to reluctant readers and connoisseurs of middle school jokes." —*School Library Journal*

SUPER SCHNOZ

and the INVASION of the SNORE SNATCHERS

GARY UREY

pictures by keith frawley

ALBERT WHITMAN & COMPANY
CHICAGO, ILLINOIS

Library of Congress Cataloging-in-Publication data is on file with the publisher.

Text copyright © 2014 Gary Urey
Pictures copyright © 2014 Albert Whitman & Company
Pictures by Keith Frawley
Pictures on vi, 16, 43, 56, 66 by Ethan Long
Hardcover edition published in 2014 by Albert Whitman & Company
Paperback edition published in 2015 by Albert Whitman & Company
ISBN 978-0-8075-7561-1

Printed in the United States of America
10 9 8 7 6 5 4 3 2 1 LB 20 19 18 17 16 15

Cover design by Ellen Kokontis

For more information about Albert Whitman & Company,
visit our web site at www.albertwhitman.com

For MJ, Gary Sr., and Don—**G.U.**

Big honking thanks to Michelle, Genevieve, Rachel, and Kaelin. Without you, life would STINK!—**K.F.**

CHAPTER 1

WEAKNESS

Every superhero has a weakness," TJ blurted out one day while Vivian, Jimmy, Mumps, and I were sitting inside our secret hideout, the Nostril.

The morning sky was bright blue and the air was already hot and sticky. Summer vacation was almost over. My friends were back from their camps and my smell tour of the surrounding countryside was an amazing success. I had added sixty-four new odors to my scent dictionary and managed to go the whole summer without getting sunburn on my nose. (My mom had stocked up with several hundred gallons of SPF 500 sunscreen.)

"What weaknesses are you talking about?" I asked TJ.

"You know, like how Kryptonite makes Superman shrivel like a worm on sizzling asphalt."

"And how Aquaman turns belly up if he's out of water for more than sixty minutes," Mumps added.

"Don't forget Wolverine," Jimmy said. "The Muramasa Blade completely destroys his self-healing powers."

Vivian, who had been playing with her pet gecko, Mr. Sticky, looked up. "That's nothing," she said. "What about Janet van Dyne—aka the Wasp?"

"What about her?" Jimmy asked.

"Her weakness is the Blob, who ate her in *Ultimatum*, Issue Two, and then remarked she tasted like chicken!"

For the next ten minutes, Vivian and the Not-Right Brothers argued back and forth about which superhero had the weirdest weakness: Thor letting go of his hammer for more than one minute; Venom, Spider-man's nemesis,

2

and his vulnerability to extreme heat; Power Girl's negative reaction to natural elements; and the Green Lantern's strange aversion to the color yellow.

While my friends jabbered away, I reached up and grabbed my Super Schnoz costume off its hanger. I took a huge whiff of the fabric. The tantalizing odors of my last Super Schnoz adventure made the hairs inside my nose tingle. Even though it had been two months since our battle with ECU, I still smelled the rancid odor of burning Stryker combat vehicles, the pungent pastrami sandwich rotting away on Mr. Toby's desk, and the disgusting fragrance of Muzzle's aftershave lotion—an astringent mix of rubbing alcohol and menthol.

But most of all, my ultrasensitive, bloodhound-like scent membranes inhaled the nasty nasal sensations of the Gates of Smell.

"What's your weakness, Schnoz?" TJ asked.

I shrugged my shoulders. "Maybe it's cayenne pepper. Snorting six bottles of the stuff nearly burned away my nasal lining."

"Cayenne pepper isn't your weakness," Mumps joked. "It gives you power the way rays from the sun fuel Superman's superhuman hearing, strength, and X-ray vision!"

Vivian and the Not-Right Brothers cracked up.

"Don't worry," Vivian reassured me. "I know that stuff wasn't good for your nose. Hopefully, you'll never have to arm yourself with cayenne pepper again. But if you do, you need to carry a spray bottle of saline solution to moisten the inside of your nasal passages after every blast."

"Schnoz will need more than a spray bottle to moisten that huge honker!" TJ squealed. "He'll need a whole tanker truck full of the stuff!"

"Very funny," I said sarcastically. "If it wasn't for my nose, you'd be floating downstream on a smelly river of SPOIL. ECU would have destroyed our school, town, and possibly the entire world."

Vivian gently picked up Mr. Sticky, placed him back inside his plastic mini-rainforest habitat, and closed the lid. "I don't know Schnoz's weakness, but I know the town's weakness. And it has nothing to do with sniffing pepper," she said.

I shot Vivian a confused look. "What are you talking about?"

She wiggled her finger, indicating I should follow her. "Let's go for a ride," she said. "The evidence is right under your nose in downtown Denmark, and you're not even aware of it."

CUP OF JOE

Vivian, the Not-Right Brothers, and I hopped on our bikes and cruised down the street. There's no way my nose could have missed something. After all, my greatest strength was the mighty booger blaster in the center of my face. The protruding proboscis had the power of flight and was capable of delivering a pepper-crusted snot missile so powerful that it could destroy a whole fleet of armored tanks. (Just ask the losers at ECU!)

Tall mountains surrounded the town of Denmark on all sides. The downtown area consisted of Main Street and a few smaller side lanes. I had explored all of them while searching out new smells for my mental scent dictionary.

Vivian's bike brakes squealed to a halt in front of Sleepy Joe's Coffee Shop.

"What are we stopping here for?" Jimmy asked.

"Look around, Schnoz," Vivian instructed. "Tell me what you see."

I scratched the tip of my nose, wondering what point she was trying to make. "I see a coffee shop and a bunch of stores," I said.

"I see the same thing," Jimmy said.

"Okay. Then tell me how *many* coffee shops you see?"

TJ started counting. "One…two…three… six…ten…eleven…twelve. There are twelve coffee shops on Main Street."

"Schnoz, when you moved here last September at the beginning of the school year, there were two coffee shops in town," Vivian said. "Since then, ten new ones have opened up. Don't you think that's a little strange?"

I shrugged. "People just like their cup of morning joe, that's all."

Vivian let out an exasperated sigh. "Ugh! Then

please tell me the names of some other businesses besides coffee shops."

"The Soundproofing Emporium," I said.

"And the White Noise Outlet," Jimmy said.

"Ear Plugs 'R' Us and the Earthquake Emergency Bargain Bin," Mumps added.

"Don't forget about the North American Seismological Laboratory that just moved into the old toothpick factory," TJ chimed in.

"What's that place all about?" Mumps asked, wiggling his loose bottom tooth. "I don't even know what 'seismological' means."

"Seismology is the study of earthquakes," Vivian replied. Then she turned to me and pointed to the shoppers strolling down Main Street. "Take a look at those people's faces," she said. "What do you see?"

I flared my nostrils and then took a good look at them. They were grown-up men and women. They all looked exhausted with big bags under their eyes.

"They look like they haven't slept in weeks," I said.

"Exactly!" Vivian exclaimed. "And what would cause people to not sleep?"

I just stared at her, not knowing how to respond.

"Noise!" Vivian yelled. "Loud racket in the middle of the night that keeps people up. That's why there are so many new coffee, ear plug, and soundproofing places in town."

"What's your point?" I asked.

Vivian stepped up to me and tapped the end of my nose. "You are my point," she said. "Schnoz, you are the world's loudest snorer! You are the reason people aren't getting enough sleep! Every night the power of your snoring causes a small earthquake that registers a 4.5 on the Richter scale, and it's getting worse. Why do you think a scientific laboratory that studies geological disturbances moved to town?"

"I've never once heard myself snore!" I fired back.

"No one hears themselves snore because they're asleep when it happens," TJ said.

"Um...Vivian's right, Schnoz," Jimmy said. "You do have a bit of a snoring problem."

"If I'm such a loud snorer," I said, "then why didn't someone tell me a long time ago? Or when my family first moved here?"

Vivian, Mumps, TJ, and Jimmy stared at the ground, like they were ashamed to answer my question.

"Because your snoring has become the town's cash cow," Vivian said finally.

"If it wasn't for your snoring," Jimmy said. "Main Street would look like a ghost town with abandoned shops and boarded-up windows. As far as this town is concerned, your snoot is an economic engine."

"Well, I find it hard to believe that you four knew about my snoring and never told me about it," I said.

"Because at first your snoring was kind of funny," Vivian said. "It was like the rumble of a distant evening thunderstorm. But over the last few months it has gotten a lot worse."

"It's true, Schnoz," TJ said. "There is a direct correlation between the escalation of your snoring, a seismological lab coming to town, and all the new coffee shops opening for business."

I couldn't believe what I was hearing! My nose felt like someone had sucked it dry with a vacuum hose. I was shocked, confused, and downright angry. I shifted my bike into gear and peeled out, racing as fast as could toward home.

CHAPTER 3

A CURE FOR SNORING

My parents were still at work when I wheeled up the driveway. I parked my bike and walked into the house. Mom and Dad had done extensive renovations in the last six months. I hadn't paid much attention to all the construction until now.

They'd had the entire foundation of the house reinforced with thick concrete. Workers had added steel frames to some of the walls. Mom had secured all of the heavy mirrors and pictures tightly. Dad had strapped all of our bookcases and cabinets to the walls to prevent overturning. He had even bolted down the refrigerator to keep it from toppling over. Stuffed away in a cabinet under the kitchen sink was a huge duffel bag labeled *Disaster Kit*, and it was filled with bottles of water, non-perishable food, and medical supplies.

In other words, my parents were earthquake-proofing the house.

I ran upstairs and threw open their bedroom door. Scattered on top of their dresser were receipts for thousands of dollar spent at downtown stores like the Soundproofing Emporium and the White Noise Outlet. I remembered that over the past few months they had added extra insulation and padding in their room. The padding was a thick foam called *Quiet Jams*, specially designed for musical recording studios.

Mom and Dad had soundproofed their bedroom to escape from my snoring!

Lately Mom had been coming into my room at night to check on me. She never turned on the light, but just sat quietly on the edge of my bed, intently watching me for a few minutes. I'd pretended to be asleep. Now I realized she was probably worried that I would die in the middle of the night from excessive snoring.

I was just about to run into the kitchen and drown my sorrows in a glass of root beer when the doorbell rang. I threw open the door and saw Vivian standing there.

"What do you want?" I asked.

"We need to talk," she said and then barged through the front door and plopped down at the kitchen table.

I poured us two glasses of root beer. "I honestly had no idea that my snoring was so bad," I said. "I wish somebody had told me."

"Have your parents taken you to the doctor lately for a check-up?"

"My mom took me for a physical a couple months ago," I said, stroking my nostrils. "But the only thing the doctor did was look inside my nose. He tried to use a normal endoscope to look up there, but it was way too small. The doctor had to rig a telescope with a spotlight so he could see what was going on way up inside my beak."

"He was probably checking for an abnormality that would cause you to snore so loudly. See, your parents *did* take you to a doctor about your snoring but didn't tell you because they thought it might hurt your feelings."

I shrugged. "Well, I never went back. So he obviously didn't find anything wrong with me."

"The thing to remember, Schnoz, is that snoring is not your fault. I've Googled the causes and there are lots of reasons. In most cases like yours, it's not a medical emergency. Loud snoring just annoys other people more than anything."

We opened up my laptop and typed "causes of snoring" into the search engine. The top four reasons were mouth anatomy, nasal problems, body weight, and sleep apnea.

"What's sleep apnea?" I wondered.

"From what this website says, it's a condition that causes the throat tissues to completely block your airway, preventing you from breathing for ten seconds or longer."

"Creepy," I said.

"Totally," Vivian agreed. "Look, let's get TJ, Mumps, and Jimmy working on this with us. We'll gather all the information on snoring cures and give them a try."

Vivian and I slapped each other a high-five and set out to find a permanent cure for my snoring.

CHAPTER 4

DUCT TAPE

The next morning, I was sitting with my mom and dad at the breakfast table. My parents looked horrible. They had dark circles under their eyes, and their faces were all red and splotchy like someone had smacked them around with a fly swatter.

"Do I have a snoring problem?" I asked, slurping down a spoonful of cereal.

Mom and Dad gave each other a weird look.

"Everybody snores, Andy," Mom answered. "Why do you ask?"

"My friends told me why Denmark has so many coffee shops and noise reduction stores in town.

It's because my snoring is so loud. Is it true?"

"You snore a little," Dad said. "But, like your mother said, everybody snores."

"But not everybody snores so loudly that it causes minor earthquakes," I said.

"Where did you get such an idea?" Mom asked me.

"I'm not stupid. I know you spent thousands of dollars soundproofing your bedroom and earthquake-proofing our house."

Mom scooted next to me. "You *do* snore, Andy," she said. "And it can be a little loud at times, but we love you and I'm sure you will grow out of it soon."

"It's kind of embarrassing," I said. "I mean, my nose is as big as a mountain, and from what I'm told, I snore as loud as a space shuttle launch."

"You're perfect just the way you are," Dad said, and then they shooed me out the door.

I met Vivian and the Not-Right Brothers inside the Nostril to plan our snoring attack. The list of cures we discovered online ranged from conventional advice—using nasal strips and taking decongestants before bed—to completely wacky things, like sleeping upside down with your feet tied to a tree limb or strengthening your throat muscles by yodeling on a hillside.

"When my dad snores at night," Mumps said, "Mom gives him a hard elbow to the ribs and then yells for him to go sleep on the couch."

Vivian rolled her eyes. "Let's start with the easiest cures," she said. "Nasal strips just might do the trick. They work by lifting the nasal passages to keep them open for normal airflow.

"Think again," Jimmy said. "Nasal strips are for people with *normal-sized* noses. Using one on Schnoz is like sticking a Band-Aid on an elephant's trunk. It won't do a thing."

"Duct tape might work," TJ mused. "It works for everything else. I read an article about a guy who made a two-story house using nothing but duct tape."

"Hmmm…" I mumbled. "I guess we could give it a try."

"Then let's do it," Vivian said. "We'll duct tape our way to a peaceful night's sleep."

Twelve-hours and sixteen rolls of duct tape later, the gang had finally managed to duct tape my nose open.

"How does it feel?" Mumps asked.

"Not very comfortable," I wheezed. "It feels like the time my nose got stuck inside a porthole when we visited the USS *Constitution* on our field trip to the Boston Navy Yard."

"There are a lot of things more important than comfort," Jimmy preached. "Like the town of Denmark getting a good night's sleep."

"How will I know if it works?" I asked.

"Simple," TJ said. "Your snoring routinely causes an earthquake that registers a 4.5 on the Richter scale. We've all felt the effects."

"Dishes break, window panes rattle, furniture topples over," Vivian added. "There could even be small cracks in the walls and foundations of older buildings. We'll ask people tomorrow if any of those things happened in the middle of the night. That's how we'll know if we cured your snoring."

"But the most important thing is the coffee shop action in the morning," TJ said. "If people are lined up down the block to get their caffeine fix, we'll know the duct tape didn't work."

Vivian and the Not-Right Brothers wished me luck and I went to bed. When the morning came, I peeled off my duct tape nasal strips and rushed around the house. I looked for broken dishes, toppled furniture, cracks in the walls. I saw no sign of damage! Hope rose in my chest like a helium balloon as I threw on my clothes, hopped on my bike, and raced downtown.

As soon as I reached Main Street, my hopeful helium balloon deflated into a lump of latex. Hundreds of people lined the streets, their eyes baggy from lack of sleep, waiting patiently for their cup of morning coffee.

I saw Vivian and the Not-Right Brothers pushing their way through the early morning cappuccino crowd. Their faces looked as disappointed as I felt on the inside.

"No big deal," Vivian said, trying to sound optimistic. "We just go back to square one and try again."

The next night, the gang talked me into taking a nasal decongestant. They were hoping the medicine would clear my nostrils and make me stop snoring. Since there was enough snot clogging up my nose to fill an Olympic-sized swimming pool, I needed to slurp down over two gallons of syrupy stuff. The experiment was a complete waste of time, money, and cherry-flavored stuffy nose medicine, because the next morning I awoke to the most damage ever. The bell tower on top of the First Parish Church had toppled over. Broken water pipes in the street spouted like Old Faithful, and even more people lined the streets for their morning coffee.

Over the next week, we tried out even more so-called cures: sleeping on my side rather than my back, sleeping on a tilted bed, exercising the muscle on the roof of my mouth, mouthpieces, homeopathic anti-snoring sprays.

Nothing worked.

The downtown coffee shops grew richer. I became more desperate.

"We've tried everything," Mumps said one day while we were hanging out inside the Nostril. "What do we do now?"

Vivian lifted Mr. Sticky from his habitat, stuck him to the wall, and stared out the window.

"What are you thinking about?" I asked her.

She turned to face me. "I hate to say it, but you may have sleep apnea."

Just hearing the word *apnea* sent shivers up my

neck. I'm not sure why, but the word sounded scary to me.

"What's sleep apnea?" Jimmy asked.

Vivian explained, "Sleep apnea is a chronic condition that causes the throat tissues to block your airway, preventing you from breathing for ten seconds or longer."

"How do we find out if that's causing Schnoz's snoring?" TJ asked.

"We do a sleep test," Vivian replied. "We rig up a camera and film him while he sleeps. The next morning we watch the film. If he has sleep apnea, we'll know exactly what we are dealing with."

CHAPTER 5

OBSERVATION

That night I felt like a monkey locked inside an animal observation lab. TJ had set up three video cameras in my room. There was one on the right side of my bed, one on the left side, and one directly above my head.

"Why do we need three cameras?" I asked.

"We need backups in case your loud snoring causes one of the other cameras to malfunction," Vivian answered.

I plopped down on my bed and covered up with a blanket. "I wish Jimmy and Mumps were here to help. Where are they anyway?"

"Mumps melted one of his sister's Barbie dolls in the microwave and got grounded for the night," TJ said.

"Jimmy had to go to his little brother's tap dance recital," Vivian added.

"That stinks," I said. "Hey, TJ, where'd you get all these cameras?"

"One is mine. The other two I swiped from my older brothers. If they find out I took them, I'm a dead man. But for you, Schnoz, it's worth the risk. All I have to do tomorrow morning is download the video from the cameras to my laptop. I'll slip the cameras back into my brothers' rooms and they'll never know a thing."

While TJ double-checked the cameras, Vivian sat on the edge of my bed and pulled out a bunch of papers from her backpack.

"What's that stuff?" I asked.

"Information about sleep apnea I printed from the Internet," she said. "We need to know what symptoms to look for. I'm glad I did some research, because the symptoms in kids and adults can be different."

I grabbed one of the pages from her and started reading.

"Bed-wetting!" I shouted. "You mean to tell me that peeing the bed is a symptom of sleep apnea?"

TJ laughed.

"That's what the medical literature says," Vivian said with a snicker.

"I can assure both of you that I have never wet the bed, even when I was a little kid."

A knock came at my bedroom door. It was Mom.

"Andy, TJ's mother just called," she said. "She wants him to come home now. And it's time for Vivian to go home. It's already dark outside."

Vivian sighed. "Well, this is it. Tomorrow morning we will know for sure if Schnoz has sleep apnea."

TJ checked the video cameras one last time, and then he and Vivian left. The room was completely dark except for the little flashing red lights on the cameras. I suddenly felt self-conscious. What if I farted or picked my butt in my sleep? The cameras would capture it all. Someone could steal the film and upload it to YouTube. The video could go viral. I'd be the laughing stock of the entire country!

I rolled over and placed the pillow over my nose. My heart was beating wildly; sweat poured down my nostrils. I lay there for what seemed like hours, tossing and turning. How could I ever get to sleep knowing three cameras were spying on my every nocturnal move?

Around midnight I heard my parents shuffle into their room and shut the door. They were in bed for the night, but I was desperately fighting the urge to fall asleep. No sleeping meant no snoring. No snoring meant I wouldn't keep the town up all night. Not keeping the town up all night meant my colossal beak wouldn't get so much extra attention.

The struggle was useless. No matter how hard I concentrated, my eyelids grew heavier and I fell fast asleep.

CHAPTER 6

SHADOW IN THE NIGHT

Rise and shine, Schnoz!"

My eyes shot open. I sat up in bed and saw Vivian, TJ, Mumps, and Jimmy standing in my room.

"What are you guys doing here so early?"

"It's not early," Jimmy said. "It's ten thirty in the morning."

I yawned and rubbed my eyes. "I can't believe I slept so late."

"You may have slept late, but the town of Denmark sure didn't," Mumps said. "Take a look out your window."

I slid out of bed and peered between the curtains. What I saw outside nearly blew my nose away. There were fallen tree limbs and debris all over my backyard. Something had toppled my next-door neighbor's chimney like a set of Jenga blocks.

"What happened?" I asked, still not believing what I was seeing.

"Your snoring is what happened," Jimmy said.

"Scientists from the Seismological Laboratory said last night's tremor was a 5.8 on the Richter scale," TJ explained.

Vivian joined me at the window. "Your snoring is getting worse," she said. "The earthquakes are becoming more destructive. If this keeps up, Denmark and maybe the entire state of New Hampshire could become one massive sinkhole."

"Don't worry," Mumps said, slapping me on the back. "I don't care what they're whispering downtown, we won't let them make you move."

The room grew silent. Vivian and the Not-Right Brothers had worried looks on their faces.

"What do you mean *make me move?*" I asked.

The gang hemmed and hawed for a few seconds, and then Vivian finally spoke up.

"There will be a special town council meeting in the next few days," she said. "That's when they'll vote whether to kick you and your family out of Denmark."

"From what my dad told me," TJ said, "the damage caused by your snoring is becoming more costly than all the money the coffee shops and noise-reduction stores are raking in."

I held my nose in my hands and felt like crying.

"But my honker saved this town!" I roared. "ECU and Muzzle were about to destroy everything! They can't kick me out!"

"We still have time to fix your snoring before the vote," Vivian said. "Let's check out the video we took last night of you sleeping. If it's sleep apnea, we can go to a doctor to fix you up."

Sleep apnea. Video cameras. With the news of my possible banishment, I had forgotten all about last night's experiment.

"Your snoring messed up the two cameras on either side of your bed," TJ said. "But, amazingly, not the one hanging above your head." He hooked a cable from the camera to his laptop. After downloading for a minute, the video was ready to watch in full HD.

I had absolutely no idea how boring watching a video of me sleeping could be.

"I can't take much more of this," Jimmy said six hours later.

"Tell me about it," Mumps said. "Melting Barbie dolls in the microwave is a thousand times more fun."

Vivian pulled Mr. Sticky from her pocket. "Stop complaining or I'll sic my assault gecko on you."

"I don't get it," TJ said, scratching his head. "We've watched nearly all of this tape and Schnoz hasn't made one little peep of a snore."

"Just fast forward to the end and get it over with," I suggested.

"Rewind to the part where Schnoz farts and picks his butt in his sleep," Mumps said. "That was hilarious!"

TJ laughed. "That's my favorite part!" Just as he was about to hit rewind, the entire screen momentarily went black, as if a huge storm cloud had passed over my room.

Vivian sat up and pointed to the screen. "Stop it right there!" she squealed. "What was that dark shadow?"

What happened next was like something from a horror movie.

"Ahhhhh!" Jimmy screeched in terror. "It's a ghost...a demon..."

"Hush up!" Vivian scolded. "We're trying to watch."

34

I gazed in wide-eyed dread as the shadow circled my bed. Slowly, the dark mass molded into the shape of a solid figure. The being was about four feet tall with wrinkly gray skin. The head was unusually large in proportion to the rest of its body, with huge eyes and small openings for the mouth, nose, and ears.

"OMG!" TJ squealed. "It's an alien from outer space!"

Two large hoses appeared in the alien's long, bony hands. The space creature then lubricated the ends of the hoses with a green, mucus-looking substance and shoved them directly up my quivering nostrils.

On the tape, I flailed and groaned but was still obviously asleep. My nostrils flared wide and I started snoring, loud snuffling snorts that made the walls of my bedroom shake.

The alien looked directly into the camera with its dark, soulless eyes. The picture grew fuzzy and then went completely black.

CHAPTER 7

NASAL VIOLATION

There was a loud thump behind me. I spun around and saw Mumps sprawled on my bedroom carpet. He had passed out cold. After waking him up by throwing a glass of cold water in his face, we watched the video again.

"This is the creepiest, freakiest, scariest thing I've ever seen in my life," Jimmy said.

"Not to mention the grossest," TJ added. "What did that alien stick up your nose, Schnoz?"

"How do I know? I was fast asleep during the whole thing."

"Does your sneezer hurt?" Vivian asked.

I shook my head. "No. But take a look inside my nostrils and see if that thing implanted some kind of alien seed or something."

Vivian and the Not-Right Brothers (except Mumps, who was sitting cross-legged on the floor, still recovering from his fainting spell) each took turns examining the inside of my nose for possible alien implantation.

TJ flicked on a flashlight and peered inside one of my nose holes. "I don't see anything out of the ordinary," he said.

"Just a bunch of crusty boogers clinging to your nasal lining," Jimmy said, looking up the other nostril.

"You guys are completely overlooking something," Vivian said.

"What's that?" I asked.

"The clue is not *what* the alien stuck up your nose. But what happened *after* it stuck something up your nose."

The Not-Right Brothers and I looked at one another with confused expressions.

"Explain," Jimmy demanded.

Vivian hit the Play button. "Let's watch it again and I'll show you."

"Do we have to?" Mumps mumbled, still looking a bit queasy.

"Yes," Vivian answered. "Now, everybody watch carefully."

We all huddled around the laptop, watching as the alien materialized from the dark cloud and proceeded to shove the hoses up my pie sniffer. I winced at the thought of an alien inserting foreign objects into my nasal cavity while I slept.

38

When we had finished watching the video three times in a row, Vivian closed the lid of the laptop. "Did you guys see what I saw?"

"I don't know what you're getting at," I said.

"Duh! Schnoz, you weren't snoring until that thing stuck the hoses up your nose!"

Jimmy pumped his fists and leaped about four feet in the air. "She's right!" he screeched. "The alien's hoses are what's causing Schnoz to snore!"

"Exactly!" Vivian beamed. "Now we need to find out why an alien enters Schnoz's room at night and shoves hoses up his nose just to make him snore."

"Maybe we should call the police," Mumps said. "We'll show them the video and then they'll alert NASA or something."

"That's a *great* idea," I said sarcastically. "Anybody with the right special effects software can fake a video these days. The police would never believe us and we'd get in trouble for making a phony report."

"But if we don't do something about the real cause of your snoring," Vivian said, "the people in Denmark will drive you out of town like some snoring witch in a thirteenth-century European village."

I sat up, rubbed my nose, and paced around the room. All this talk of aliens, hoses, and snoring was making my boogers ache. I just wanted to slip on my Super Schnoz costume and fly away from it all.

"We just need to sit down and come up with a plan," Jimmy said.

"Then let's go back to the Nostril and figure something out," TJ said.

"Guys, this isn't like fighting the ECU," I pleaded. "They were human beings just like us. How can we possibly stop an alien with higher intelligence from nasally violating me every night?"

The room grew silent. Everyone was confused and a little bit scared—especially me. As far as I was concerned, the task was nearly impossible.

"Well, Schnoz," Vivian said. "This situation affects you the most. What should we do?"

"I'm really confused right now," I said, my

thoughts tumbling clumsily inside my head like a preschool gymnastics class. "I need to get outside, take a good sniff, and inhale all of this before I can do anything."

I ran out of the house, hopped on my bike, and took off down the street.

CHAPTER 8

THE CENTER FOR UFOS, EARTHQUAKES, AND ALIEN ABDUCTIONS

I didn't stop pedaling until I reached the Nostril in Jimmy's backyard. I spun the code on the combination lock and stepped inside. A blast of heat hit me like a hot pizza oven. Our secret hideout wasn't air-conditioned and the place was like a sweaty sauna on a hot summer day. Vivian must have left Mr. Sticky out of his cage, because the gecko was stuck to the windowpane, soaking up the sunshine.

My Super Schnoz costume was dangling in the corner on a coat hanger. I hadn't worn the outfit since defeating ECU. I slipped off my clothes and stepped into the suit. A box of Mardi Gras masks with beaks sat in the corner. I picked one out and slid it over my nose. This one had a plume of bloodred feathers and a glittery paint job. The beak was metallic silver with adjustable black straps.

I was one fancy-looking turkey buzzard!

A breeze rattled the trees in the backyard. I positioned myself in the middle of the grass as a huge gust of air shot up my nostrils. Instantly, they inflated like the wings of a giant wandering albatross. My stomach leaped into my throat, my toes lifted off the ground, and my cape flapped in the breeze.

I was flying!

The town of Denmark stretched out below me like a village in a toy train set. I inhaled deeply and banked hard to the right, heading toward the White Mountain National Forest (WMNF) outside of town. The WMNF was almost a million acres, and within the park were four federally protected wilderness areas. That meant there were no roads or houses in the forest, and the only people were occasional hikers. The area's remoteness offered just the kind of solitude I needed to contemplate my alien problem.

That was when I caught a pungent whiff of something tantalizingly fishy. The smell was a combination of rotting bait and burning ammonia so intense it made my nose hairs stand on end. I scanned my mental scent library for a match. Nothing. The smell was completely new to my olfactory receptors. I had to find its source!

Closing one nostril with my finger, I began my descent into the WMNF. The closer I got to the ground, the more intense the smell became. I skimmed the treetops until I came to a clearing in the forest. To my wide-nosed surprise, I saw some kind of compound. There were two small trailers, a massive, globe-like structure with the lens of big telescope popping from the roof, an above-ground swimming pool, and a smaller structure about the size of my dad's garage. That was where that awesome smell was coming from. I had to find what was causing that odor!

I landed softly on an old logging road and walked stealthily toward the garage. Along the path, a hand-painted sign staked into the dirt read: *The Center for UFOs, Earthquakes, and Alien Abduction—Dr. Aðalbjörn Wackjöb, Director.*

A hoard of hungry mosquitoes buzzed around my nose. I shooed them away and kept walking. When I got to the garage, I peered into its dirty windows. I didn't see anybody, but the source of the smell was as plain as the nose on my face. Hanging like giant spider egg sacs were row after row of some kind of drying meat. Next to the Gates of Smell, this nasty jerky was the most horrifyingly delicious glop I had ever smelled in my life.

Quietly, I gripped the door handle and walked inside. The smell hit my cookie detector like a megaton stink bomb. It was as if I had died and awoken in stench heaven!

45

I grabbed two hunks of the rancid meat and held them to my nostrils. The rancid smell drove my nose crazy. My nostrils flared; my scent receptors quivered in ecstasy. I forgot all about aliens and snoring and basked in the pure joy of smelling!

The garage door flew open. I spun around and saw an older man with wild gray hair and a white lab coat. He was holding a loaded shotgun.

"Get your hands off my hákarl," the man growled with a thick, European-sounding accent.

I held up my hands. "S-s-sorry," I stuttered. "I was just…"

"What are you doing here?" the man interrupted. "Why are you wearing that costume and ridiculous-looking mask? Are you with the government?"

The old guy had just asked me three questions in a row. I didn't know which one to answer first, so instead I hurled the meat I was holding at him and made a break for the door. The man fired at me. I braced myself for the shotgun blast. But instead of bullets, all I got was water.

He wasn't holding a real gun. It was just a fancy water pistol!

Once I got outside, I inhaled a hard gust of wind and sailed into the clouds. I looked down. The old man was watching me fly away, firing rounds of water into the sky.

CHAPTER 9
THE REYKJAVÍK REVIEW

When I arrived back at the Nostril, Vivian and the Not-Right Brothers were waiting for me.

"Where have you—" Jimmy started to ask, and then pulled his shirt over his nose.

"Holy stinky skunk, Schnoz!" TJ cried out, plugging his nostrils.

"You absolutely reek!" Mumps gagged.

Vivian handed me my street clothes, "It's the Super Schnoz costume that smells," she said. "Go outside and change."

I stepped behind the nostril and took a huge whiff of my cape, tights, and shirt. They smelled exactly like the malodorous meat hanging inside that old guy's garage.

"I don't know what you guys are so upset about!" I yelled from outside. "That smell is awesome, second only to the Gates of Smell in my opinion."

"We're not letting you back inside until you change!" I heard Vivian shout through the wall.

I peeled off my suit and plopped it in the grass. Within seconds, the smell had attracted a swarm of green poop flies (technical name: bottle fly). Poop flies were my favorite insect. Next to dogs, they were the only ones who loved stinky, rotting things as much as I did.

So as not to nasally offend my friends any further, I took a shower with a garden hose before slipping back on my street clothes.

"What nasty substance were you rolling in?" Mumps asked me when I went back inside.

"Some kind of meat," I replied.

"Were you spending time at the roadkill butcher shop?" Jimmy joked.

"No," I answered. "The meat was actually

hanging from a peg, drying inside a building deep inside the WMNF."

"Explain," Vivian ordered.

I told the gang the whole story, from flying over the WMNF, smelling the meat, to almost getting my head blown off by a crazy old guy with a high-powered water gun.

"I wonder why a person would be living that far out in the woods." Vivian said.

I shrugged my shoulders. "Don't know. But he was some kind of scientist. There was a sign along the path heading to his property that said *The Center for UFOs, Earthquakes, and Alien Abduction*. The guy's first name was long with a bunch of squiggly lines over the letters. His last name was Wackjöb, with two dots over the *o*. Dr. Somethingorother Wackjöb."

Vivian scratched her chin, thinking. "Hmmm…" she muttered. "TJ, would you please fire up your laptop and Google *UFOs, alien abduction, Dr. Wackjöb*."

TJ typed in the search and hit Enter. He scrolled through a bunch of pages before finding something relevant. "This may be something," he said. "It's an old article from the *Reykjavík Review*—Iceland's English Newspaper."

We huddled around the computer and read.

Doctor Defends UFO Research
By Sigudur Bödvarsson

REYKJAVÍK, Iceland—The well-respected seismologist, Dr. Aðalbjörn Wackjöb has been accused of misappropriating money from the University of Iceland's Geology Department where he had been Chairman. This week Karí Thordarson, University President, fired Dr. Wackjöb for the unauthorized funding of his controversial UFO earthquake theory.

The investigation looking into Dr. Wackjöb's activities has been ongoing for the past eight months. University officials feel they have unearthed enough evidence to terminate the doctor's tenure. "UFOs are the cause of the entire world's seismic activity!" Dr. Wackjöb shouted to reporters as police led him away from his office. "My scientific research will prove it!"

What Dr. Wackjöb calls science, others call "just plain kooky," according to several of his colleagues inside the University's Geology Department. Dr. Wackjöb has also become a laughingstock in the scientific and academic worlds with his claims that aliens are abducting thousands of people (mostly children) each year and using them in their extraterrestrial earthquake experiments.

Dr. Wackjöb, who also has an advanced degree in astronomy from the Ludwig-Maximilians-Universität München in Germany, plans to relocate to the United States to continue his UFO, earthquake, and alien abduction studies.

"That was his first name," I said. "*A...owl... bee...yourn*, or however it's pronounced. The sign said Aðalbjörn Wackjöb."

"Do you think it's the same man, TJ?" Vivian asked.

TJ turned to me. "What was the name of his center again?"

"The sign said *The Center for UFOs, Earthquakes, and Alien Abduction—Dr. Aðalbjörn Wackjöb, Director.*"

"It has to be the same guy," Jimmy said. "How many Aðalbjörn Wackjöb's can there be who study UFOs, earthquakes, and alien abductions?"

"I one hundred percent agree," Vivian said. She then produced a flash drive from her pocket and plugged it into the USB port of TJ's laptop.

"What are you doing?" TJ grumbled, miffed that Vivian was touching his computer.

"I'm transferring the video of Schnoz and the alien from the computer to the flash drive."

"Why would you do that?" Mumps asked.

Vivian peeled Mr. Sticky from the window and gently stroked the reptile's head. "Because Schnoz is living evidence of Dr. Wackjöb's theory and the video proves it."

CHAPTER 10

GRÍÖARSTÓR NEF

Vivian had a dentist appointment that afternoon, so we had to wait until the next morning before heading to see Dr. Wackjöb. I went to bed that night sniffling with anxiety. TJ had hooked up the camera system to get another video, but the whole thing still freaked me out. I smuggled a two-liter bottle of soda into my room and chugged it down before bed, hoping the caffeine would keep me awake. The idea was a complete waste of high-fructose corn syrup and carbonated water. By the time midnight rolled around, I couldn't keep my eyes open.

The morning came and it was clear there had been another earthquake. This one was a 6.0. The walls of my bedroom were slightly cracked and my dresser had toppled over.

"The town's in an uproar, Schnoz," Mumps said when the guys arrived at my house. "There's damage to a lot of houses. People are really angry."

"We have to get you out of town," Jimmy said. "It's for your own safety."

While I got dressed, TJ downloaded the new video from the camera to his laptop, and then to the flash drive.

"Let's watch it," Mumps suggested.

"No time," TJ said. "We have to meet Vivian and then get to Dr. Wackjöb's compound ASAP."

Vivian was waiting for us when we got to the Nostril. She was holding up a brand new Super Schnoz costume.

"Where'd you get that?" I asked.

"I made it for you last night," Jimmy said. "Your old one was way too smelly so I threw it in the garbage."

I ran inside the Nostril and slipped on my

new suit. It was the exact same color as my old one—black tights, black shirt, blue cape, and blue Super Schnoz emblem. Jimmy had added a utility belt with hidden pouches to hold jars of cayenne pepper, spray bottles of saline solution, and an electric nose hair trimmer.

"It's a bird, it's a plane, it's Super Schnoz!" I cried, jumping around the corner.

"Let's get a move on," TJ said. "We need to see this Dr. Wackjöb."

"How are we going to get there?" Mumps wondered. "It'll take hours to ride our bikes way out there."

Vivian dragged out the harness I had used to fly everybody onto the school rooftop during my battle with ECU. The stitchwork Jimmy had done on the fabric was still perfect, right down to the feathers that made it look like a pregnant turkey buzzard.

"We're not riding our bikes," Vivian said. "Schnoz is going to strap on the harness and fly us all there." She slipped five jars of cayenne pepper and two spray bottles of saline solution into my new utility belt.

"What's this stuff for?" I asked her.

"Just in case," she said. "You never know what we'll run into way out there."

"Like Bigfoot!" Mumps screeched.

Vivian rolled her eyes as she and the Not-Right Brothers crawled into the harness. I secured the belts to my back, slipped on my Mardi Gras mask, and was ready to fly. The wind wasn't very brisk, so we had to wait for me to get enough air inside my nostrils for takeoff. When my nose finally inflated to its full glory we were off, sailing into the sky toward Dr. Wackjöb's compound deep in the WMNF.

The smell of the rotting meat guided my way. After thirty minutes of flying, I made a perfect landing on the path leading to the UFO Center.

"See the sign," I said, pointing. "It's over there, stuck in the ground."

"*The Center for UFOs, Earthquakes, and Alien Abduction—Dr. Aðalbjörn Wackjöb, Director*," Jimmy read. "If this guy can't help us, then no one can."

I pulled off the harness and hid it in the bushes. "Like I told you," I said, "the old guy is kind of loony. He asked me if I was from the government."

"Sounds paranoid to me," Mumps said. "And a little—"

"I don't blame him," Vivian interjected. "After getting fired from his job, the man has trust issues."

Jimmy laughed. "You sound like a therapist. Maybe you should make him lie on a couch."

Just as Vivian opened her mouth to fire a volley back at Jimmy, we all heard a loud crack in the nearby woods.

"What was that?" Mumps cried out.

I pressed a finger to my lips, hushing everyone up. We all grew as silent as dandelions and listened for more sounds.

There was nothing.

"Maybe it was a moose or a black bear," TJ whispered.

Jimmy shrugged his shoulders. "Whatever it was, it's gone now."

And that's when a cannon blast of frigid water hit me full force in the stomach. The water

pressure was so powerful it knocked me off my feet and sent me nosefirst into a thick maple tree. My Mardi Gras mask flew off my head and landed on a branch above my head. Vivian and the Not-Right Brothers got the same treatment. The intense surge of water sent them flying a good ten yards into a stand of white pine.

When I came to my senses, I saw Dr. Wackjöb emerge from the woods dragging a fifty-foot-long fire hose.

He looked at Vivian and the Not-Right Brothers. "That's what you get for trespassing!" He then turned to me, an angry scowl on his face. "And as for you, Gríðarstór Nef, that was for ruining two hunks of my precious hákarl!"

CHAPTER 11

ROTTEN SHARK MEAT

I reached for my bottle of cayenne pepper, ready to sneeze Dr. Wackjöb back to the Paleozoic Era, but Vivian stopped me.

"Stop spraying us!" Vivian shouted. "We have proof that aliens exist!"

Dr. Wackjöb lowered the fire hose. "What kind of proof?"

"A video," TJ said. "The kid you called *Gríðarstór Nef*—whatever that means—has been visited by aliens. They shove big pipes up his honker and make him snore."

A look of skepticism washed over Dr. Wackjöb's

face. He held up the hose, like he was going to water blast us again. "I've been laughed at and shunned by the scientific community," he said bitterly, "I won't allow a bunch of children to make fun of me too."

"We're not here to make fun of you," Vivian pleaded, and then plucked the flash drive from her pocket and tossed it at Dr. Wackjöb's feet. "Plug this into your computer and watch it for yourself," she said. "It's a video of weird aliens doing some nose experiment on Schnoz."

Dr. Wackjöb picked up the flash drive, rubbing it gently with his fingers like it was a precious diamond. He looked at us, back down to the flash drive, and then back at us again. "What are your names?" he asked.

"Vivian."

"TJ."

"Mumps."

"Jimmy."

"Andy," I said. "But my friends call me Schnoz."

"Or, if you get on his bad side," TJ added, "he'll become Super Schnoz and pepper-sneeze you all the way back to Iceland. This guy's whiffer has the power to blow up a fleet of armored tanks and blast an eighteen-wheeler in half."

Dr. Wackjöb stared at my nose for a long second. "I like the name *Grïöarstór Nef* for you better. Follow me. My computer's in the observatory."

All of us looked like dripping wet rats as we trekked to the observatory.

Vivian handed me my mask. "Here," she said. "You're not Super Schnoz without your disguise."

"I might as well leave it off now," I said. "Dr. Wackjöb's seen my face so what does it matter?"

The Not-Right Brothers and Vivian plugged their noses as soon as we stepped into the compound.

"That smell is disgusting," Jimmy choked.

"It reeks like your gross old Super Schnoz suit," Mumps gagged.

"That's the building where he dries the meat," I said. "The place is full of the stuff."

"Ask him what it is," Vivian said.

I broke away from the gang and caught up with Dr. Wackjöb. "Excuse me, but can you tell me about that meat drying in that building? What's it called again?"

"Hákarl," Dr. Wackjöb said, not breaking a stride. "It means *rotting shark* in the Icelandic language. It's a delicacy in my country served at the midwinter Þorrablót Festival."

My nostrils flared wide. Any food that started with the word *rotting* made my nose hairs tingle with delight. "How do you make it?" I asked.

Dr. Wackjöb explained the fine art of hákarl-making as we walked. A butcher kills, guts, and debones the shark. He then leaves the meat to rot in a hole covered with stones for two months. After that, he dries the meat in a well-ventilated room for another two months. The Hákarl is then ready for eating.

"Why do you let it rot?" I wondered. "I mean, why not eat it fresh?"

"Sharks that live in the waters around Iceland are poisonous," Dr. Wackjöb answered in his funny accent. "Those sharks don't have urinary tracts like you and me. That means they must secrete their urine from their skin. The high amounts

64

of uric acid in the meat are so concentrated that eating it can cause people sickness. If you allow the shark to decay, the urine is naturally removed from the flesh making it digestible."

I looked over my shoulder to see if Vivian and the Not-Right Brothers had caught Dr. Wackjöb's hákarl explanation. From the sickly green expressions on their faces, I could tell they heard every word.

The observatory was a lot bigger than I had remembered from my first visit. The place had a round roof and was as large as a four-story building. When we walked inside, I saw computers, printers, and other beeping gadgets that looked so hi-tech I didn't know what they were for.

Above our heads was something extraordinary.

"The glass is beautiful," Vivian said with a hint of awe in voice.

"Like something from a church," Mumps said.

"What you are looking at," Dr. Wackjöb explained, "is a telescope mirror that allows me to see ten billion light-years into the universe. I call it the Cosmoscope, and the viewer can observe planets that orbit distant suns. I have seen new planets form in spectacular supernova explosions."

"This is the most amazing thing I have ever seen in my life," TJ said, his mouth hanging open in wonderment.

"Where did you get the glass for the lens?" Jimmy asked.

"I made it myself," Dr. Wackjöb said with pride.

Vivian's eyes lit up. "How'd you do it?"

We listened intently to Dr. Wackjöb's every word as he described the fascinating process. "I heat chunks of glass in a large furnace at two thousand degrees Fahrenheit," he explained. "The glass melts into a syrupy liquid and then drains into a large mold. The glass takes ninety days to cool enough for the finishing touches."

"How do you make—" TJ started to ask, but Dr. Wackjöb cut him off.

"Enough questions for now," he said. "I want to see this video."

I snatched the flash drive out of the seismologist's hand. "No one sees this video until you answer my question," I said, my nostrils flaring. "What does *Gríðarstór Nef* mean?"

CHAPTER 12

PLANET APNEA

Gríöarstór Nef means *vast nose* in Icelandic," the doctor explained.

In an instant, the Not-Right Brothers were laughing so hard that tears rolled down their cheeks.

"We should have called you Super Gríöarstór Nef!" TJ guffawed.

"Very funny," I said sarcastically. "I wonder what loser translates to in Icelandic."

"Loser is *tapar* in my native language," Dr. Wackjöb said.

"Knock it off, you guys," Vivian ordered. "All

four of you are *tapars* as far as I'm concerned. Let's watch the video so we can get down to business."

I handed the flash drive back to Dr. Wackjöb and he connected it to his computer. The video started to play and his already pale complexion grew even paler when the creepy shadow materialized into an alien on the screen. I winced inside as the little gray nose-molester shoved the hoses up my two sniffers.

When the video ended, Dr. Wackjöb was speechless. He sat up, walked over to the Cosmoscope, and sat there in silence for what seemed like an hour.

"Um…excuse me, Dr. Wackjöb," Vivian said. "Aren't you going to tell us what you think of the video?"

"It's…it's…" Dr. Wackjöb stuttered. "Utterly amazing. It's the concrete proof I have been searching years for."

"Then why do you seem so upset?" Mumps asked.

"I'm not upset. I'm just stunned because four American children found the proof before me, a highly educated scientist."

69

"Who cares who found it," I said. "The question is what are we going to do about it?"

"We have another one," TJ said.

"Another what?" Dr. Wackjöb asked.

"Last night's video of Schnoz sleeping."

"Then let's see if our vast-nosed friend had another alien abduction."

When Dr. Wackjöb said the words "alien abduction," a cold shiver went up my nose. I had never thought of my experience in those terms before. But that was my reality. I was the unconscious victim of a human nose experiment conducted by aliens from outer space.

The first six hours of the video were all the same—me sleeping—so Dr. Wackjöb fast-forwarded until we saw the first wisps of a shadow form above my bed. It took all of my courage to keep watching. I mean, who knew what the aliens were going to shove up nose next?

"This is the same thing that happened the night before," Vivian said.

Dr. Wackjöb pressed a finger to his lips,

70

indicating for everyone to be quiet. This time, the shadow formed into *two* aliens. They were identical with tiny slits for noses and mouths and huge eyes. The hoses they used for my nose were twice as large as they'd been the first night. When the aliens shoved them inside my nostrils, I flailed so much that a third alien materialized from the dark cloud and held me down.

Then the snoring happened: loud, rumbling snorts that shook the room and made my dresser topple over. A small crack fissured its way up my wall. The aliens turned and looked at each other. Their once dark, soulless eyes now beamed with a fluorescent green light.

I heard a loud thump directly behind me. Mumps had passed out again.

"They're communicating with each other," Jimmy said.

"I bet they're talking about how big Schnoz's nose is," TJ said. "Or about all his boogers."

"They're Apneans," Dr. Wackjöb muttered.

"That's exactly what I thought too," Vivian said. "Schnoz has a horrible case of sleep apnea."

Dr. Wackjöb shook his head. "I said *Apneans*, not apnea. Follow me to the Cosmoscope."

Dr. Wackjöb turned on a switch, played with some knobs, and the farthest corners of the universe, looking as if they were only inches away from our faces, popped up on a giant screen. The celestial sky twinkled like someone had spilled a jar of silver glitter onto black construction paper.

A series of *oohs* and *ahhs* went up from Vivian and the Not-Right Brothers. Dr. Wackjöb positioned the mouse on his computer and a flash of light in the middle of deep space appeared on the screen.

"Is that a star?" TJ asked.

"No," Dr. Wackjöb replied. "It's a planet, proof that other life-forms exist in the universe. I have named it Apnea."

"Why Apnea?" I wondered out loud.

"Apnea comes from the Greek, meaning *to breathe*," Dr. Wackjöb explained. "The study of this planet is my living breath. It is all I live for. That is why I have named the planet Apnea. Watch as I zoom in closer."

The screen grew fuzzy for a moment and then became as clear as a green booger on a white tissue. Mountain ranges, lakes, rivers, buildings, and UFOs flying through the planet's airspace came into view.

"Wow," Vivian said. "This is just like looking at Google Maps, but instead of a neighborhood you can see a whole planet."

"Gríðarstór Nef," Dr. Wackjöb said to me, "this is the planet Apnea, four billion light-years from Earth. Home of the aliens that are snatching your snores."

CHAPTER 13

SNORE DESTRUCTION

W̲e have to let the world know!" TJ shouted. "This is the greatest discovery in the history of mankind!"

Dr. Wackjöb looked at TJ with a frown. "Young man, I have informed NASA, the British Interplanetary Society, the Russian Space Federation, and even a Wal-Mart security guard," he said bitterly. "I sent them the exact galactic coordinates of my planetary discovery. No one believes me enough to bother looking."

"Can you zoom in closer?" I asked.

With a press of a button, the Cosmoscope

focused in on the planet Apnea. We saw thousands of aliens that looked just like the ones who shoved hoses up my nose. The extraterrestrial beings seemed to be hovering around a large, metallic-looking object.

"What's that thing they're working so hard on?" Vivian asked.

"Not sure," Dr. Wackjöb answered. "It is partially obscured by a reflective light shield. Do you see the planet's two suns in the distance?"

We nodded our heads.

"As the planet revolves around the suns, the Apneans will move the light shield. Perhaps then, we can get a glimpse of their laborious project."

"I want to see it now," Jimmy groaned.

"Have patience, my boy. Our planet revolves every twenty-four hours, but Apnea revolves every two hours. That's how long we have to wait until they move the light shield."

For the next one hundred and twenty minutes, we listened as Dr. Wackjöb explained his theory of UFOs, earthquakes, and alien abductions. With the video of the spacemen sucking snores from my booger maker, his work was no longer a theory, but a proven fact.

"Gríðarstór Nef," Dr. Wackjöb said to me, "Apnea is in trouble."

"What are you talking about?" I asked.

"Our world derives its power mostly from fossil fuels," Dr. Wackjöb explained. "Apneans, on the other hand, have no such resource. They use solar power originating from their two suns."

Vivian scratched her head. "I can't wrap my brain around this," she said. "What do solar power and Schnoz's snoring have to do with each other?"

"Look at their two suns on the screen," Dr. Wackjöb instructed. "Tell me what you see."

"I see two big red suns that pulse every few minutes," Mumps said, still looking a bit nauseous from his latest blackout.

"That is an excellent observation. Although our own sun looks yellow, it is actually white. Only when the sun's light passes through Earth's atmosphere does it change from white to the yellow color we see. That is the sign of healthy, relatively young sun."

"Thanks for the science lesson," I said impatiently. "What's your point?"

Dr. Wackjöb turned to look at me. "The point is that a sun nearing the end of its life throbs like a giant heart. It runs out of hydrogen fuel at its core like a motorcycle engine runs out of gas. It also turns a brilliant bloody red, just like the two suns of Apnea."

"So their two suns are dying," Vivian reasoned. "Without a sun they have no solar power. Without solar power they…"

"They find another place to live," Dr. Wackjöb interrupted. "When Apnea's suns die, the planet will die. Its inhabitants are acutely aware of this. The Apneans need Gríðarstór Nef's snores for destruction." Dr. Wackjöb's face grew gravely serious. He looked me in the eye and said, "The Apneans have been harvesting more and more of your snores to use against us. They will use your nose to cause earthquakes and destroy our civilization. Their master plan is to invade Earth and then build a new world in their own image."

"Good-bye, Earth; hello, Apnea," Mumps muttered.

Vivian pointed to the screen. "Look!" she yelled. "The Apneans are moving the light shield!"

Everyone stared at the screen. I watched in horror as the aliens pulled away the light shield and revealed the most disturbing, the most frightening thing I had ever seen in my life.

"It's...it's..." Jimmy stuttered, but the words got stuck in his throat.

Mumps collapsed in a fleshy lump at my feet. Vivian gaped in wide-eyed astonishment. Dr. Wackjöb just looked on with a serious expression on his face.

"It's an enormous spaceship shaped like Schnoz's honker!" TJ cried. "They created a giant Robo-Nose to destroy the world!"

CHAPTER 14

ROBO-NOSE

From the screen, Robo-Nose looked like a ten-story-high, five-school-bus-wide replica of my beak, right down to the shape of my bristly nose hairs. I watched as hundreds of Apneans climbed inside the mechanical muzzle. Moments later, a thrust of snore-fueled, boogery snot exploded from the metal nostrils like a thousand rocket blasts. Robo-Nose slowly rose off the ground, hovered in midair, and then shot through the atmosphere and out of sight.

"They are coming for us," Dr. Wackjöb said. "They have powered their nasal ship with

Gríðarstór Nef's snores. They will then fly around to different parts of the earth and cause massive earthquakes to destroy our planet. This is just as I predicted but no one would believe me!"

"How long will it take for them to get here?" Vivian asked.

Dr. Wackjöb punched some numbers into a computer program. "Apnea is four billion light-years from Earth. If my calculations are correct and Robo-Nose is traveling at the speed of snores, it should take them two solar days to reach our planet."

"A solar day is twenty-four hours," TJ said. "They'll be here on Saturday."

"That stinks!" grumbled Mumps. "I was supposed to go to fishing on Lake Winnipesaukee this Saturday with my uncle. But now it looks like I'm going to have to help save the world from an alien invasion."

"Well, get over it!" Jimmy barked in Mumps's face. "If Apneans take over Earth you'll never go fishing again—because you'll be DEAD!

"Knock it off, you two," Vivian ordered. "We have to come up with a plan or we're all goners."

"Vivian is right," I said. "It's up to us to save the world." I turned to Dr. Wackjöb. "And how exactly will we accomplish that?"

"We fight fire with fire," Dr. Wackjöb said. "Or, in your case, we fight nostril with nostril. Is it true that you blew up army tanks and large trucks with just your nose?"

"Absolutely!" I announced proudly. "Well, with the help of a snoot full of cayenne pepper. Do you want to see what it can do?"

Dr. Wackjöb nodded and we walked outside. Luckily, Vivian had reminded me to bring a bottle of pepper. At the back of the compound were six massive boulders. I knew from school that retreating glaciers from ten thousand years ago had left them behind. I took a huge sniff of cayenne, aimed, and sneezed with all my snot. The boulders shot off the ground like golf balls smacked from a tee and then exploded into a million pebbles.

"Astonishing!" Dr. Wackjöb gushed. "That nose of yours is as a lethal weapon!"

"Now we know exactly why the Apneans picked Schnoz," Jimmy said.

"Without a doubt, young man. I think we just may have a fighting chance against these invaders. Your proboscis is one of the most powerful forces on Earth."

We filed back into the observatory and planned our next move. While Dr. Wackjöb crunched numbers into his computer, trying to determine the exact coordinates of the alien landing, Vivian, the Not-Right Brothers, and I talked things over. The first thing we addressed was my nightly visits by little gray space men. The more snores they harnessed, the more power they had.

"Let's ambush them when they materialize from that dark shadow," Vivian suggested.

"What do you mean?" TJ asked.

"You guys have a sleepover at Schnoz's house. When the aliens appear to do their hose-up-the-nose ritual, you grab them and tie them up as prisoners."

"That's stupid," Jimmy said. "What are we supposed to do with them after we tie them up? Hold them for ransom until they agree to leave our planet alone?"

"We should just conk them over the head," Mumps said, flailing around like a ninja ready for battle. "One quick karate chop to the skull and they'd be history."

"Mumps, you pass out just seeing them on video," I said. "If you saw an alien in real life, you'd probably spontaneously combust. As far as I'm concerned, Vivian's on the right track."

"How so?" Jimmy asked.

"You guys saw the aliens on tape. They're about our size. Jimmy, do you think you can sew up a couple alien costumes?"

"Schnoz, that's a brilliant idea!" Vivian beamed. "We should tie up the real aliens and then dress up like them. That way we can go on board Robo-Nose and sabotage it from the inside."

I slapped Vivian a high-five. "Exactly right. Wrap them up in duct tape. That stuff is good for practically everything."

"The dark shadow is some kind of passageway that transports them to our world and then back to Robo-Nose, their main booger ship," TJ said. "We just have to enter the shadow in place of the real aliens."

Jimmy paced around the room, thinking. "It sounds like a good plan to me, but who is going to take the trip from the shadow to Robo-Nose? This is a lot riskier than just sneaking into our school to battle ECU."

"There's no way I'm doing it," Mumps said. "I'll stay down here on solid ground and work with Dr. Wackjöb."

Vivian looked at Jimmy and TJ. "Then it's up to us, partners. It can't be Schnoz because he has to battle them nostril to nostril from the outside."

She looked at her watch. "Schnoz, you better fly us home so Jimmy can stitch up some alien costumes. It looks like we're going to have a busy night ahead of us."

Just as we had done when we first formed our crime-fighting superhero team, we all bent over until our noses were touching.

"On the count of three," I said. "One, two, three..."

"*Gríöarstór Nef!*" we all screamed.

SLEEPOVER

After an hour of begging, my mom and dad reluctantly agreed to allow Jimmy, Mumps, and TJ to sleep over. Of course, Vivian couldn't spend the night because she's a girl, but we had that all figured out. The two of us would be in constant walkie-talkie communication. When the Not-Right Brothers and I had subdued the aliens, I'd let Vivian know and she would sneak over to my house. She, Jimmy, and TJ would then slip on the alien suits and disappear into Robo-Nose.

"This is the fastest sewing job I've ever done in my life," Jimmy said when he got to my house that night.

"Let me see your work," I asked, anxious to see his creation.

"Don't worry, Schnoz," TJ said. "You're going to be impressed by our fashion artist friend."

Jimmy yanked out the three costumes from his gym bag. The outfits were awesome, right down to the silver-colored material to the slits for the mouth and nose.

"Where'd you get the material?" I asked.

Jimmy smiled. "I raided my older sister's dresser drawer of all her spandex dance clothes. They were all black, so after I finished stitching the get-ups together, I found some silver spray paint in the garage and gave them a couple coats."

"Let's try them on," Mumps suggested.

Jimmy, TJ, and Mumps slipped into the costumes. They looked exactly like the little aliens who had been snatching my snores. In fact, they looked so real I wanted to reach out and cuff them a good one upside the head.

"Mine fits like a sock," Jimmy said.

"This one feels good too," TJ added.

Mumps strutted around my room, making

alien noises. "Since Vivian is about my size, it should fit her perfectly. While you guys are inside Robo-Nose, I'll be working with Dr. Wackjöb. Schnoz can fly me there in the harness."

A knock came at my bedroom door.

"I have some cookies and hot chocolate for you boys."

It was my mom.

Jimmy, TJ, and Mumps quickly ripped off the alien costumes.

"Thanks, Mom," I said, opening the door and taking the plate of goodies.

"Don't you boys stay up too late," she said. "Understand?"

"Okay," we mumbled through a mouthful of cookies.

When my mom left the room, I looked at the clock sitting on my nightstand. "It's nine thirty already," I said. "I'm checking in with Vivian."

I pressed the red button on the walkie-talkie. "Vivian. Can you read me?"

"Roger that," Vivian replied, her voice full of static.

"I saw the costumes Jimmy made. They look just like the real thing."

"Good. I'll be drinking soda full of caffeine to stay awake. Remember, when the cloud appears you have to let me know. Then I'll sneak over to your house. Okay?"

"Sounds good," I answered. "I'll make sure the back door is unlocked so you can get inside. Over and out."

"What do we do now?" Mumps asked when I turned off the walkie-talkie.

"Let's play a few games of Electronic Battleship and then go to bed," TJ suggested.

Jimmy slurped down the last drop of his hot chocolate. "I won't be able to sleep," he said.

"Me either," I agreed. "But we have to turn out the lights. If the aliens don't think I'm asleep, they may not come."

The Not-Right Brothers and I played a few rounds of Electronic Battleship until around midnight.

"I guess it's time," TJ said.

"You got that right," I said, crawling into bed and flicking off the light.

Jimmy, TJ, and Mumps unrolled their sleeping bags on the floor and slid inside. The only sounds were the occasional fart by Mumps, followed by a round of raucous laughter. My eyelids felt as heavy as bowling balls, but I fought the urge to sleep. The Not-Right Brothers, on the other hand, gave in to the sandman too easily. Soon, all three of them were crashed out, thin lines of drool dripping from their open mouths.

I tossed and turned in my bed, trying to stay awake. My discipline paid off. As the crimson-colored numbers of the alarm clock flashed 4:00 A.M., I felt a gust of warm, heavy air pass over my body. My eyes squinted in the semidarkness. I saw a dark shadow forming above my bed.

"Jimmy, Mumps, TJ!" I shout-whispered. "Something's happening."

"Huh…" Jimmy mumbled in his half-sleep.

"Whatta…?" TJ muttered, turning over in his sleeping bag.

A pungent electrical smell filled the room. I watched as

the shadow slowly molded into the shape of two little gray aliens. The space invaders hovered at the foot of my bed, staring at me with large dark eyes, each holding a flexible hose the size of a sewer pipe.

CHAPTER 16

INTO THE SHADOWS

I reached for the walkie-talkie. "Vivian! They're here!" I yelled.

Before I could say another word, the aliens lunged at me. They shoved a hose up each nostril. Instantly, I began to snore, a loud, grinding snivel that made the walls of my bedroom shake and the coffee can full of pennies on my dresser crash to the carpet.

The aliens' dark eyes beamed with fluorescent green light. They were communicating with each other, but I had no idea what they were saying. One of the aliens waved a lightning-bolt-shaped wand over my head. Suddenly, the room started spinning; my brains rattled against the sides of my skull. I felt like they were sucking my insides out through my nose!

"Do...do...do something..." I managed to utter to my friends. But they just stood there (except for Mumps, who was still crashed out in his sleeping bag, completely oblivious to what was going on) with their mouths hanging open, fear etched on their faces.

My bedroom door swung open. I looked up and saw Vivian. She dove at the aliens and managed to tackle one to the ground.

"Yuck!" Vivian cried out. "They're all slimy and slippery!"

Jimmy leaped into action. He grabbed the other alien and shoved him to the ground.

"And they smell too!" Jimmy shouted.

The alien Vivian was holding slithered from her grasp and came at me again. He gripped both hoses and shoved them deeper into my nostrils. I writhed in pain, begging my friends to help me. This time TJ lunged at the spaceman, ripping the hose from the alien's bony hands and pinning the snore thief to the ground.

"Duct tape them!" I yelled to Vivian. "Before they get away!"

Vivian went to work, wrapping each Apnean in layers of silver duct tape. While she secured the bad guys, TJ flicked on the lights and gently pulled the hoses out of my nose.

Mumps rolled over in his sleeping bag. "Did the aliens come?" he asked, rubbing the sleep from his eyes.

"Take a look," I told him.

Mumps sat up, took a long gander at the duct-taped aliens, and then conked out cold.

The aliens' eyes lit up like a Fourth of July fireworks show. They were communicating with each other, so Vivian shut them up by blindfolding them with a strip of duct tape.

"That should keep you Apneans quiet for a bit," she said.

"What should we do with them?" TJ asked.

I shrugged my shoulders. "Don't know."

"Let's haul them back to the Nostril," Vivian

suggested. "We don't want Schnoz's mom waltzing inside his room only to find two space aliens wrapped in duct tape."

"Great idea," I said. "We'll carry the slimy buggers out of the house before my parents wake up."

"Ahem…" Jimmy grunted, and then pointed to the floor.

I looked down and saw for the first time how the Apneans stored my snores. They used some kind of large metal box that looked like a battery. Connected to the battery were the two hoses. The power of my snores went through the hoses and into the battery.

"What do we do with that stuff?" TJ asked.

"Bring it back to Robo-Nose," Vivian said, slipping on one of the alien costumes.

Jimmy and TJ looked at each other with the same uneasy expressions on their faces.

"Do you mean that we should still try to infiltrate Robo-Nose?" Jimmy asked.

"Of course," Vivian said. "That was the plan. Now get on your alien outfits."

Jimmy and TJ reluctantly pulled out their costumes and started to change. That's when the light in the room dimmed like a storm cloud passing over the sun.

"It's the shadow," Vivian gasped. "Get on your costumes before it disappears!"

The shadow was actually beautiful, almost hypnotic in a strange way. The shady gloom wasn't distorted, but clear and crisp like a shadow puppet against a white screen. I lifted my nose, wondering if the thing had any smell, when some invisible force grabbed hold of my nostrils.

"Help!" I cried out. "Something's pulling me by the nose into the shadow!"

Vivian jumped onto the bed and grabbed my leg. She tugged with all her might, but her effort was useless. The vacuum was too powerful.

"Someone throw me an alien costume for Schnoz to wear!" Vivian shouted. "Hurry! Before it's too late!"

Jimmy ripped off his costume and tossed it to Vivian. The suction doubled in force, inhaling Vivian and me along with the hoses and battery

CHAPTER 17

THE OLFACTORY BULB

into the dark depths of the shadow.

The intense pressure of the shadow propelled Vivian and me through a long tunnel. The journey felt like being inside a giant neon glow stick. A fluorescent green hue—the same shade as the Apneans' eyes when they communicated with each other—illuminated the passageway as we traveled into another dimension.

I looked up and saw that we were heading straight for an even brighter light. Vivian and I clutched each other's hands as we burst through a thin snot bubble and landed feetfirst in a small room.

"Where are we?" I wondered.

Vivian shrugged. "I have no idea."

The wheezing sound of Robo-Nose's snore-propulsion system hummed in my ears. A wall behind me began to shimmer like a precious jewel. I saw the outlines of three Apneans forming in the cascade of colors.

Vivian pulled on her alien mask and tossed me my costume. "Put this on before they materialize!"

The alien outfit Jimmy had stitched together fit me nice and snug, but the mask was another story. The thing wouldn't fit over my nose!

"Help me!" I hollered to Vivian. "They're almost visible!"

Vivian yanked at the mask, trying with all her might to slip the disguise over my beak. "This is like a grown man trying to put on a four-year-old's sock," she grunted. "On the count of three, we'll give one giant tug. One…two…three…!"

The mask slipped over my nose just as the Apneans appeared in the room. Without even acknowledging us, they picked up the snore hoses and battery storage and then scurried away.

"What should we do now?" Vivian asked.

"We need to stay under the radar and try to find the ship's weakness," I said. "Remember, these creatures are out to destroy Earth."

Vivian handed me another jar of cayenne pepper. "Just in case," she said, and then we walked through the shimmering door and into Robo-Nose.

We walked down a long corridor. The walls were metallic colored, and every few yards were weird glistening doors. The Apneans barged in and out of them without giving us a second glance.

"I think our costumes are working," I said.

"Let's go in one of the doors and check things out," Vivian suggested.

"Um…are you sure?" I hesitated. "What if we walk through a door and it's an Apnean ladies' restroom?"

Vivian brushed me off. "These aliens are highly advanced beings. They probably don't even have genders or go to the bathroom."

I took a deep breath and we stepped through a door. The experience was like taking a shower with rainbow water. Brilliant colors washed over us as we materialized on the other side. We saw two Apnean heads behind a privacy wall. Their eyes were flaming with fluorescent green light, obviously in deep conversation with each other. The Apnean closest to us reached up and pressed a button. A loud whoosh like a toilet flushing filled the room. My nose caught a whiff of a stinky, familiar scent.

"What's that bad smell?" Vivian whispered to me.

"Apnean poop," I said. "This really is an alien bathroom."

Before the other Apnean could flush his space age potty, Vivian and I rushed back into the hall.

"There goes your theory that Apneans don't have bodily functions," I said.

She ignored my comment and kept walking. After exploring for a bit, we discovered that Robo-Nose was broken up into three levels: the lower Nose Hair, the middle Mucous, and the upper Olfactory Bulb.

"The Olfactory Bulb is where we want to be," I said. "That's the nerve center of this operation."

"How do you know?" Vivian asked.

"Trust me. I know my nose, and this whole spaceship is a giant replica of my pie sniffer. The Olfactory Bulb's job is to transmit smells from the nose to the brain. That's why dogs and I have such superior senses of smell. Our Olfactory Bulbs are quadruple the size of a normal human."

"Let's go," Vivian said, and we headed for the upper level.

Robo-Nose's Olfactory Bulb was brimming with activity. Apneans hustled back and forth, their eyes afire with green light. A viewing deck with a giant glass screen peered into endless space.

"Do you see that blue dot in the distance?" Vivian asked.

"Yes," I said back. "Do you think it's Earth?"

"Absolutely. Look behind you."

I turned around and saw a screen with a map of the planet Earth. Three important-looking Apneans were pointing at the screen, zeroing in on North America. They zoomed in closer until only the state of New Hampshire popped up on the screen. After another quick magnification and the town of Denmark and the surrounding woods appeared in plain view.

"That's where they're headed," Vivian said. "Our little town."

"I hope Dr. Wackjöb is watching Robo-Nose's descent to Earth on the Cosmoscope," I said.

A flurry of activity broke out behind us. Vivian and I turned and saw a bunch of anxious-looking Apneans surround another large screen. We watched with dread as my bedroom popped up on the display. A movie played out before our eyes, showing the Not-Right Brothers fighting the snore-sucking aliens, and Vivian and me disappearing into the shadow.

The Apneans had recorded the whole scene.

CHAPTER 18

RUNNING FOR OUR LIVES

A loud, flashing alert signal blasted from the intercom system.

Vivian grabbed my hand. "They know we're on the ship," she said, panic gripping her vocal chords. "Let's get out of here and figure out what to do next."

We nonchalantly walked out the Olfactory Bulb so as not to draw any unwanted attention and disappeared down the hall.

"What are we supposed to do now?" Vivian asked when we got to the Nose Hair level.

I brushed away the bristly, booger-crusted hairs that were dangling from the nasal lining ceiling. "I have no idea," I said. "But we're not leaving until we can figure out this flying snot machine's weakness."

Vivian paced back and forth, thinking. "Weakness…weakness," she muttered out loud. "If this ship is an exact design of your nose then it must have the same weaknesses as you."

"We went over this a few days ago. My nose doesn't have any weaknesses."

"Remember that day you got hit in the snoot by a dodgeball in PE class?"

"Of course I do. My honker bled so bad that the nurse alerted every bloodmobile in the state. I single-handedly supplied every hospital in New England with a year supply of type O positive blood."

"What if we figured out a way to cause Robo-Nose to have a massive nosebleed?"

"Not very likely unless you can find a dodgeball the size of the moon."

Vivian pulled up her mask and looked me in the eye. "We have to think of something fast," she said. "One of two things is going to happen very shortly. Either the Apneans are going to find us and kill us, or they're going to land on Earth and destroy the planet."

The options didn't sound good to me.

"There's one nice thing from this experience," I said.

"Like what?" Vivian grunted.

My nostrils flared and my scent receptors tingled with pleasure. "All the new alien smells for my scent dictionary," I took a long, deep sniff. "The Apneans' stinky odor, their tangy poop, and the perfume of the strange shimmering doors. I love all these new smells!"

Vivian's eyes grew as big as softballs. "That's your weakness!" she shouted. "Smells!"

I raised my eyebrows, not understanding what she was trying to say. Then it slowly dawned on me. *Smells* were my weakness and my strength all wrapped into one!

"You are a genius!" I told her. "Robo-Nose and I have the same weakness—smells!"

"Exactly. What's the smelliest thing you have ever smelled?" she asked.

"The Gates of Smell," I answered.

"Okay, then what's the *next* nastiest thing you have ever whiffed? There's no way we're ripping up the gym floor and exposing that nasty pit."

I thought for a second. Dog poop smeared on the bottom of a sneaker, crusty unwashed underwear, burning human hair, rotting roadkill, my dad's farts, Principal Cyrano's body odor, foot fungus...

"Rotting shark meat, without a doubt," I decided.

Vivian's face crinkled in disgust. "Hákarl! The rotting shark meat soaked in its own urine."

"Somehow we have to lure Robo-Nose with the smell of hákarl and..."

Before I could finish my sentence, I looked up and saw several Apneans rushing toward us. Their big alien eyes lit up like fireflies.

"They see us!" Vivian squealed.

"How do they know it's us?" I asked.

"Your mask is ripped!"

I reached up and felt the fleshy cartilage of my schnozola. She was right. The fabric in the mask

had torn open and my nose was popping out
like a clown from a jack-in-the-box. An Apnean
raised a lightning-bolt-shaped wand and aimed it
directly at us. We both ducked as a spray of light
shot from the end and exploded above our heads.

"They're shooting!" Vivian cried. "Run!"

I took a quick sniff of pepper and sneezed a
round of cayenne-fueled snot right at them. The
boogery phlegm smacked into an invisible shield
and then ricocheted harmlessly away.

"The cayenne pepper isn't working," I groaned.

Vivian and I rushed down several hallways, the Apneans in hot pursuit.

"Let's find the portal back to your bedroom," Vivian said, huffing for breath.

We burst through a bunch of shimmering doors, searching for the way back home. The more rooms we ran into, the more Apneans joined the chase. A blast from one of their lightning wands clipped my left nostril and sent me spiraling to the floor.

"Owww!" I cried. "They shot my sniffer!"

Vivian held my nose in her hands. "It's just a scratch," she said. "There isn't any blood. Let's go!"

We were running for our lives, the Apneans closing in fast. I could smell their stinky skin and poopy behinds. My nostril throbbed with pain. Just as I was about to fall over from exhaustion, we burst through a shimmering door and saw the portal back home.

"This is it!" Vivian hollered.

"Are you sure?" I asked.

"It looks the same. Anyway, we have no choice. The Apneans are…"

Four armed aliens charged into the room. They aimed their lightning wands directly at us. Before they could fire, Vivian and I dived through the snot bubble and into the glow-in-the-dark tunnel.

CHAPTER 19

SWEET DREAMS

We were falling, tumbling end-over-end through a vast void of nothingness. Below us was a bright light. I closed my eyes, praying the light was coming from the nightstand in my bedroom.

Vivian and I burst through the snot bubble and landed on top of my bed. We bounced off the mattress directly on top of Mumps, who was still fast asleep in his sleeping bag.

"Get off me," Mumps grumbled.

"Where were you guys?" Jimmy asked. "One minute you're here and the next minute you're gone."

"Schnoz, your nose is all red," TJ said.

I looked in the mirror and saw a huge red scrape on my left nostril. The wound was sensitive to touch and felt like the brush burn I had gotten on my leg once from sliding down a playground pole in shorts.

"The Apneans shot at me," I said.

"Tell us everything," Jimmy demanded.

For the next twenty minutes, Vivian and I explained our journey into the mucous depths of Robo-Nose. From the shimmering doors, the Apnean bathroom, to the nerve center inside the Olfactory Bulb, and my theory about Robo-Nose's weakness—smells.

"How could all that happen when you were only gone for one minute?" Jimmy asked.

"We were gone for hours," Vivian said.

"No you weren't. You guys disappeared into the shadow on the ceiling for a few seconds and then came back."

"That's impossible," I muttered.

Jimmy pointed to the clock on my nightstand. "It's four twenty in the morning. I looked at the clock right after you guys disappeared into the shadow. The time was four nineteen."

"Space-time continuum," TJ said. "Einstein came up with it. His theory says the universe has three dimensions—up and down, left and right, forward and back. There's also a fourth time dimension, and that's called the space-time continuum. It basically means that space time is different from Earth time."

A rustling sound came from the corner of my bedroom. I looked over and saw the two duct-taped Apneans. I had completely forgotten about them!

"What are we going to do about—" I started to say when the shadow appeared once again on my ceiling.

"They're coming for us!" Vivian screeched.

We all watched as the shadow hovered above the Apneans. A loud sucking sound filled my room, and in flash of bright light, the aliens rose in the air and disappeared into the shadow.

"That takes care of that problem," Mumps said, sliding out of his sleeping bag.

"What should we do now?" Jimmy asked.

Before I could answer, a knock came at my door.

"Andy!" My mom said, raising her voice. "It's late and time for you boys to settle down. Understand?"

"Sorry," I said. "We'll go back to bed."

Mom's slippers padded down the hallway. After her bedroom door shut, I whispered, "When Vivian and I were in Robo-Nose's control room, we saw a giant map of Denmark. That means they're landing right here in New Hampshire to start the first phase of their global invasion."

"And we know that Robo-Nose is flying at the speed of snores," Vivian added. "They're going to land soon, probably sometime this afternoon or tomorrow at the latest."

"Plus," TJ said, pointing at Vivian and me, "They are going to be looking for you two."

My heart plunged into my stomach. From the look on Vivian's face, I could tell she felt scared too. I hadn't been this afraid since Vivian and I swan-dived into the Gates of Smell.

"Super Schnoz," Vivian said. "You are the only person who can save us."

"Blow them to smithereens with the cayenne cannon!" TJ cheered.

"Pepper sneezes have no effect on them," I said, patting a jar of cayenne strapped to my belt. "I tried it when the Apneans were chasing Vivian and me. They have some kind of invisible shield that deflects the snot."

"Just like Magneto from the X-Men," Mumps said. "He has a force field that can block out matter and energy. The field is strong enough to withstand a hundred nuclear bombs."

"Except that there is a big difference between Magneto and the Apneans," Jimmy said.

"What's that? Mumps asked.

"Magneto is a fictional comic book character and Apneans are real!"

"Shhhhh!" I hissed, pressing a finger to my lips. I don't want my mom to wake up again."

"The reflective shield they possess means we can't fight them with conventional sneezes," Vivian said.

"Then how are we supposed to destroy them?" Jimmy asked.

"We need to lure Robo-Nose to Dr. Wackjöb's compound with the stinky hákarl."

"Why?" TJ asked.

"Robo-Nose is Schnoz's evil doppelgänger," Vivian explained. "We all know that Schnoz can't resist stinky smells. That means the giant booger factory snoring its way toward Earth loves nasty scents too."

I walked over to the window and looked outside. The first winks of dawn peeked over the WMNF. Summer was ending; school would be starting soon, and that meant fall allergies. I was severely allergic to pollen from plants belonging to the genus Ambrosia—otherwise known as ragweed. I could already feel my nose tingling, eyes itching, and gallons of snot pouring from my honker. The ragweed made my sinuses throb and ears plug up so bad it felt like my head was going to implode.

"I got it!" I screeched.

"Got what?" Vivian asked.

"I know how we can defeat Robo-Nose! We plug up its nostrils so the thing implodes from the inside!"

I heard my mom's bedroom door open. Her feet stomped angrily down the hallway toward my bedroom. Vivian hid under the bed, I jumped under the covers, and the Not-Right Brothers slipped into their sleeping bags.

"Sweet dreams," Mumps chimed, and then we all pretended to be asleep.

CHAPTER 20

STAGING AREA

The next morning, Vivian and the Not-Right Brothers met me inside the Nostril. I put on my tights, cape, Mardi Gras mask, and instantly became Super Schnoz!

"Schnoz, your idea to plug up Robo-Nose's nostrils is good," Jimmy said. "But how can we pull it off?"

"That flying snotter is massive," Vivian said. "There isn't enough ragweed on the whole planet to stuff that muzzle up."

"We have to think of something," TJ said.

"What about Krazy Glue?" Mumps suggested.

"It would take enough Krazy Glue to fill up Lake Winnipesaukee to close up that metallic honker," I said. "The thing is massive."

Vivian paced around the Nostril, thinking. She peeled Mr. Sticky from the window and stroked his rough, leathery skin. "Did you know that a gecko's sticky toe pads are so strong they can hold the weight of two adult males?"

"So?" Jimmy grunted. "What's your point?"

"I don't have a point," Vivian said. "I was just saying."

"I read all about geckos," TJ said. "They have tiny hairlike thingies called *setae* on the base of their toes. Over two million setae could fit neatly on a quarter. Their feet are one of the stickiest substances on the planet."

"Maybe we can use Mr. Sticky to plug up Robo-Nose," Vivian said.

"That's a great idea!" Jimmy said sarcastically. "Let's go round up a billion geckos and shove them up Robo-Nose's booger factory."

"It was just a suggestion," Vivian fired back. "I don't hear you coming up with any ideas."

"Let's talk to Dr. Wackjöb," I said. "Maybe he knows what to do." I popped my nose out the door and took a sniff. "The wind is picking up. It's a good time to fly."

Vivian and the Not-Right Brothers positioned themselves in the harness. I pulled the straps tight, a gust of wind inflated my nostrils, and we were sailing into the sky. We were cruising at an altitude of two thousand feet when I saw something large punch through Earth's atmosphere.

"Look at that big plane!" Mumps gushed.

"That's not a plane," I heard Vivian say. "It's Robo-Nose."

I watched as the flying snout speeded toward the WMNF, the rumble of my stolen snores powering its humongous nostrils. Robo-Nose was an invincible snoring machine. The massive mechanical mucous maker made me quiver with anxiety. I would have to fight my evil twin nose-to-nose and nostril-to-nostril in an epic battle to save Earth.

Would I have enough nose power to do the job?

"Fly faster, Schnoz!" Jimmy shouted.

Robo-Nose descended like a cruise missile into the forest outside of town. A huge blast of green booger bombs shot from its beak followed by a massive explosion. Trees, rocks, and other debris exploded into the sky.

"That thing just blew up Dr. Wackjöb!" Vivian cried.

From a trick I learned from watching a TV show about peregrine falcons, I pinned my arms at my sides and dove at breaknose speed toward Dr. Wackjöb's compound. We came within a few hundred feet and my nostrils spread wide. A familiar, tangy stench tingled my nose hairs—hákarl. The round dome of the Cosmoscope was still intact.

"Robo-Nose didn't blow anything up!" I shouted to my friends. "I see the Cosmoscope and smell the rotting shark meat!"

"Then what did that thing just destroy?" Jimmy asked.

"I'm going to drop you off at Dr. Wackjöb's compound and find out," I said.

I deposited my friends off and then did a

reconnaissance flight. Robo-Nose had blasted a clearing in the woods about five miles from our present location. Dozens of Apneans buzzed around like flies on a dead squirrel. They were clearing away fallen trees and brush, preparing a staging area for their world conquest.

They assembled what looked like a row of army barracks and a large storage building for supplies. Space-age-looking land rovers rolled out of Robo-Nose, carrying two massive hunks of metal shaped like rectangles. The Apneans placed the blocks on top of each other. But they didn't touch. They just hovered in midair like two magnets repelling each other.

I knew from science class that magnets also draw things together. Robo-Nose fired up its snore engines and hovered between the two floating magnets. Instantly, the space nose's nostrils started flaring. The ground below quaked with tremors. I was just about to turn and fly away when a fleet of booger-shaped blobs flew out of Robo-Nose.

The booger blobs were vehicles the size of

large jellyfish. Two weapons that looked like torpedo launchers were at their sides. The blobs positioned themselves in battle formation and test fired at the surrounding pine trees. Lethal, laser-like nose hair rockets shot from their guns, blasting the towering trees into toothpicks.

A rocket ricocheted off a large rock and then beelined in my direction. I managed to duck out of the way, but the rocket's tailwind made me bank sharply to the left. The gust of sudden wind caused my butt to rise in the air, and, like the rudder on an airplane, made me pitch downward into a descent. I inhaled with all my might, desperately trying to gain altitude, but it was no use.

I was crashing nosefirst into Robo-Nose's staging ground.

BATTLE OF THE
BOOGER BLOBS

I hit the ground so hard my nose was impaled by a mound of dirt. As I struggled to free myself, a sharp pain ripped through my backside. An Apnean had shot me in the butt at close range with a lighting wand!

"Owww!" I screeched and yanked my nose from the ground.

Mucky soil had packed into my nostrils like cement. My face scrunched up, my eyes closed tightly, and I sneezed. The sludge lodged inside my nose discharged directly into a platoon of Apneans. They must not have been wearing their

invisible shields, because the expulsion sent the invaders tumbling into the forest.

The Booger Blobs were on me fast. A round of nose hair rockets blasted in my direction. Before they could send me to nose-picker heaven, I inhaled a large gust of wind and soared into the sky. I attempted to outmaneuver them, but they were too fast. Remembering the Forest Moon of Endor chase scene from my all-time favorite movie, *Star Wars Episode VI*, I dived straight for the heart of the dark forest.

I dodged and ducked my way through the trees, careful of low hanging branches and fallen limbs. The booger blobs were hot on my nose. Hair rockets exploded all around me. I snorted a snoot full of cayenne pepper and shot a spicy blast right at them. Just like when I was on the Apnean ship, my snot bomb ricocheted off of their invisible shields and bounced harmlessly away.

The lead booger blob—which was a dark green color like the infected snot from a cold—soared to my rear. The thing was so close I could hear the slurping sound of its phlegm-powered engines.

Click...click...

The sound of the booger blob locking and loading its nose-hair guns was unmistakable. In an act of desperation, I scraped the forest floor with my hand and grabbed a handful of sticky pinecones. I hurled the seed cases over my shoulder directly at the booger blob.

The pinecones miraculously penetrated the deflection shield and stuck to the flying mucus like a Band-Aid. I watched as the booger blob sputtered. Snot fuel sprinkled from its tank, and it crashed to the ground in a brilliant explosion of loogies and gray-green discharge. Another booger blob raced beside me. Before the snotty thing could raise its rockets and fire, I swung my head and nudged the alien with my nose. My efforts knocked the booger blob off balance just enough for me to bombard it into submission with more pinecones.

I didn't have time to ponder why pinecones breached their invisible shields and not the Cayenne Cannon. Maybe when I speared one with a pinecone, it affected their balance and sent the slimy things into a deadly tailspin.

A nose-hair rocket blasted past my head and nearly ripped off my nose. I turned and saw two-dozen more booger blobs racing after me. Six of them were gaining on me fast. I knew I could never fight that many at once in nose-to-nose combat. So instead of throwing pinecones with my hands, I shoved them up my nostrils and fired them like missiles from a jet fighter. One by one, the booger blobs dripped away like a runny nose on a winter day.

I flew as fast as I could, inhaling deep snorts to keep up my speed and velocity. When I was sure no more Booger Blobs were coming after me, I inflated my nostrils and rose over the forest canopy.

That's when I saw Robo-Nose expel a blast of hot air from its nostrils. The rancid nasal expulsion withered vegetation and scorched the earth. The giant nose's snoring became so loud it made my ears ring. The olfactory energy made the floating magnets grow hotter. Flashes of brilliant emerald green and pink lights illuminated the sky. The light show was spectacular, like having a front row seat at the aurora borealis. I was spellbound until I looked back down at the ground.

The earth below Robo-Nose was shaking violently. A small fissure had split open the ground and was growing larger. Forty-foot high trees toppled and two-ton boulders rolled into the crack like toy marbles. I watched helplessly as the crevice slowly expanded outward in all directions.

More booger blobs appeared on the horizon. Apnean ground troops formed a column and marched along the fault line. They were heading straight toward Dr. Wackjöb's compound and then on to Denmark for the destruction of our town.

CHAPTER 22

POLYDIMETHYLSILOXANE AND
NANOTUBES

The Cosmoscope was shaking like a dog in a thunderstorm when I landed back at the compound. I rushed inside the observatory and saw Vivian and the Not-Right Brothers desperately trying to stabilize the giant telescope.

"Help us, Schnoz!" Vivian shouted when she saw me.

"Grab this strap and secure it to the wall," Dr. Wackjöb ordered.

I tugged the long leather strap and hooked it to an iron peg screwed into the wall. Jimmy did the same on the other side. After a few tightening adjustments, the Cosmoscope stabilized into position.

"Robo-Nose started an earthquake," I said, out of breath.

"I figured it was either that or a massive elephant herd was stampeding our way," Jimmy said.

"What do we do now?" Mumps asked, a look of fear in his eyes. "Are we all going to die?"

"No one is dying," I consoled him. "Not as long as Super Schnoz is still alive and sniffing!"

"What did you see out there?" TJ asked me.

I filled them in on everything, from landing nosefirst into the dirt, getting my butt zapped with a lightning wand, to my epic battle with the booger blobs. Dr. Wackjöb turned as white as vanilla ice cream when I told him about the giant magnets and the magnificent light display.

"What's happening?" Vivian asked, seeing the seismologist's concerned expression.

"The Apneans' mission to destroy Earth has begun," Dr. Wackjöb said grimly. "They will cause massive earthquakes, tsunamis, climate change, and ultimately our species' extinction."

Vivian, Mumps, and I looked out the observatory window. In the distance, I heard the awful phlegm-sucking sounds of the booger blobs' engines. The trees were shaking; the Apneans were getting closer.

"Now that we know what they're trying to do, let's come up with a plan to stop it." Vivian said.

"We already thought of a plan back at the Nostril," I told her. "Robo-Nose must be destroyed. It's like killing the queen of a beehive. Once the queen bee is gone, the hive is doomed."

"Perfect analogy, Gríðarstór Nef," Dr. Wackjöb said to me. "But even my superior mind cannot think of how we can destroy it."

"We don't need a superior *mind* to stop that extraterrestrial snot maker, we just need a superior nose!" Vivian pulled Mr. Sticky from her coat pocket. "That and my little cold-blooded friend. We already know how to destroy Robo-Nose."

I smiled at Vivian and then looked Dr. Wackjöb in the eye. "We have to plug up Robo-Nose's nostrils. If we can do that, the whole schnozola

131

will break apart like a battered piñata at a little kid's birthday party."

The floor shuddered beneath our feet. Dr. Wackjöb grabbed a door handle to stabilize himself. "You are absolutely right," he said. "Why didn't I think of that?"

"Who cares who thought of it!" Vivian hollered. "We're running out of time!"

Dr. Wackjöb stared at the ceiling, muttering to himself. "Nose, nasal passages, blockage. Congestion, allergies, head cold, nasal polyps...I got it!" he yelled.

"What is it?" TJ asked.

"We need to make some kind of synthetic mucus," Dr. Wackjöb explained. "It must be the thickest, most gelatinous substance on earth."

"The footpads on a gecko's feet make some of the stickiest substances on earth," Vivian said.

Dr. Wackjöb nodded his head. "Setae. You are absolutely right. All I would need to produce synthetic setae quickly is polydimethylsiloxane and carbon nanotubes, which I have inside my laboratory."

"What about sticky pinecones?" I suggested, and then I told him how the pinecones were able to pierce the booger blob's invisible shields.

"It probably wasn't the pinecone itself that had the penetration power," Dr. Wackjöb said. "But rather the resin surrounding the pinecone. That's another good source of stickiness."

"We have two ingredients," Jimmy said. "Synthetic gecko feet and pinecone gunk. Is that enough to make fake snot?"

"We'll need a liquid base to hold all the ingredients together," TJ said.

"You can use my own snot for a base," I offered. "It's almost allergy season and my mucus is as thick as whale blubber."

"Perfect," Dr. Wackjöb said. "Let's get to work!"

CHAPTER 23

TRAIL OF HÁKARL

D̲r. Wackjöb drained the above-ground swimming pool behind the Cosmoscope. Everyone stood back as I filled it back up with every drop of my gooey snot. The pool looked like a giant bowl of tapioca pudding topped with green raisins.

"That is plenty for the base," Dr. Wackjöb said. "Mumps, I need you to collect as many pinecones as you can carry. TJ, follow me to the laboratory. I will need an assistant to make the adherent mixture."

Mumps disappeared into the woods and Dr.

Wackjöb and TJ hurried into the laboratory. The dirt rumbled underneath our feet. Robo-Nose's angry snores grew louder. Dr. Wackjöb's compound and the town of Denmark were first in line for the Apneans' total domination of Earth.

"How are we supposed to shove fake snot up Robo-Nose's nostrils anyway?" Jimmy asked.

I shrugged. "Dr. Wackjöb will let us know."

"We need to lure Robo-Nose to us," Vivian said. "Just like in Hansel and Gretel, but instead of a trail of bread crumbs we leave Robo-Nose a trail of rotting, urine-soaked shark meat."

Jimmy plugged his nose. "Schnoz, you need to get it within whiffing distance of Robo-Nose. The smell of the stuff makes me want to throw up."

"He's right," Vivian added. "I can't go anywhere near the stuff either."

The harness I used to transport Vivian and the Not-Right Brothers to Dr. Wackjöb's compound lay crumpled in the weeds. It gave me the perfect idea.

"I load up the harness with the hákarl," I said. "I'll fly over the Apneans' staging ground and drop a hunk every twenty yards or so. Remember, Robo-Nose is an exact copy of my sneezer. If I love the luscious smell, then my mirror image will too."

"It sounds kind of risky to me," Jimmy said.

"We don't have any other choice," Vivian told him. "If the hákarl doesn't work, we'll all be dead meat just like those poor decomposing sharks."

Hundreds of hunks of Hákarl dangled on hooks inside the drying shed. I loaded as many as I could into the harness. Just as I was about to levitate into the sky, I saw the dark cloud of booger blobs getting closer. I stuffed dozens of pinecones into my utility belt in case I needed to defend myself.

"Don't forget to take some cayenne pepper," Vivian suggested.

"It doesn't work on Apneans," I said. "You saw with your own eyes."

Vivian shoved a jar into my utility belt. "Cayenne pepper is like having a Boy Scout knife. You never know when it might come in handy."

I flew low, skimming the treetops to stay out of sight of the booger blobs. Robo-Nose's snoring had ripped a chasm into the earth ten yards wide and fifty yards deep. The fissure grew longer and longer with every snort from the mighty mechanical nose. When I arrived at the Apneans' staging ground, I hovered in midair and checked out the scene.

The ground around Robo-Nose was smoking with flames. The two floating magnets were red hot; the light emanating from them was a horrific, fiery vision of Hades. I stuffed a hunk of håkarl up my nose and sneezed with all my might. The rotting shark meat landed within a few feet of Robo-Nose's throbbing nostrils.

137

What happened next made my honker hoot with joy! Slimy scent pods shot out of Robo-Nose and sniffed up the hákarl. I sneezed another piece, this time a little farther away. The massive beak rotated its nostrils and rolled toward the stinky meat. Again, the scent pods grabbed the bait and snorted it up in one sniff.

For the next forty-five minutes, Robo-Nose followed the scent of hákarl through the woods like a hungry tiger tracking a wounded goat. A legion of Apneans followed close behind their fearless sniffer. The booger blobs flocked in the sky above me. Out of the corner of my eye I glimpsed a half-dozen of them dive, firing their nose-hair rockets at the ground.

A voice screamed out, "They blew up the Cosmoscope!"

It was Vivian.

I flew as fast as I could toward Dr. Wackjöb's compound, dropping the last hunks of hákarl along the route. When I arrived, I saw little gray Apneans everywhere. The compound now looked like a war zone. Plumes of dark smoke rose over the devastation. Booger Blobs had blasted the sight into submission, destroying nearly every building. The only thing standing was the swimming pool full of my snot. I desperately sniffed the air, smelling for my friends.

A group of Apneans had captured Vivian, Jimmy, and Mumps. The enemy had bound them at the wrists and they were being marched into the woods. Dr. Wackjöb and TJ were nowhere in sight. I shoved a few rounds of pinecones up my nose and dived to rescue my friends.

Mumps looked up and saw me speeding toward him. "Super Schnoz, look out!" he screamed.

I glanced around to heed his warning. That's when two booger blobs fired at me. Three rounds missed their mark, but the fourth shot was a direct hit. A deadly nose hair pierced my right nostril and sent me spiraling out of control toward the ground.

CHAPTER 24

NOSTRIL-TO-NOSTRIL RESUSCITATION

The blast knocked me out of the air and sent me tumbling into the weeds. My wounded nostril throbbed with pain. Blood dripped from the end, soaking the Super Schnoz emblem on my chest. I inhaled deeply, sniffing to see if my smell powers were still working. The strong, stinky scent of Apneans wafted into my nostrils. I looked up and saw a gang of them racing in my direction.

I reached into my utility belt and shoved five pinecones up each nostril. As the Apneans were about to pounce on me, I pointed my honker howitzer and sneezed right at them. My aim was perfect. The pinecones pierced their invisible shields and blew them across the compound.

Across the battlefield, I watched Dr. Wackjöb and TJ climb out of an underground bunker. They were carrying a huge tub of sloshing green liquid. As the Apneans closed in on them, the two managed to hoist the tub over the rim of the pool and dump its contents. The chemical reaction between the synthetic mucus and my real snot instantly doubled the concoction like a giant batch of bread dough rising over a loaf pan.

A loud rumbling sound came from the woods. Robo-Nose had followed my trail of hákarl just as we had hoped. But how could I deliver the payload? Snaked around the swimming pool was Dr. Wackjöb's firehose. I realized his plan was to slurp the fake snot up with the hose and shoot it into Robo-Nose's nostrils.

The idea was brilliant. Except for now, Dr. Wackjöb and TJ were prisoners of the Apneans.

I fought my way to the swimming pool, firing rounds of pinecones at the pursuing aliens and their flying booger blobs. Robo-Nose had discovered the source of the hákarl supply and snorted every bit of the stinky stuff into its greedy nostrils.

What I saw next made my nose quiver with fear. The Apneans were marching my friends straight toward the alien sniffer's pulsing proboscis.

"Help us, Super Schnoz!" Vivian cried out.

Dr. Wackjöb, Vivian, and the Not-Right Brothers were within twenty yards of Robo-Nose. I had to act or lose my friends and the planet forever. I dove for the firehose. Just as I gripped it between my hands, a booger blob shot at me. The nose-hair rocket punctured the hose, shredding it to pieces. What would I do now? There was only one choice: I would have to inhale the synthetic mucus into my nose and then implant it into Robo-Nose myself.

I gripped the sides of the pool and plunged my nose into the bubbling booger brew. After a quick huff, my nostrils had sucked up every drop of the glutinous mixture. The gunk was super sticky, like Krazy Glue on steroids. I ran toward Robo-Nose and attempted to sneeze the snot into his awaiting nostrils.

Nothing came out.

The stuff had clogged up my nostrils like dry cement.

"Use the cayenne pepper!" Vivian shouted at me. "Rub it inside your nostrils with your finger. The heat of the pepper may be enough to loosen the adherent."

I grabbed the bottle and dumped some pepper into my hand. Thankfully Vivian had insisted I carry it along. I plunged my pepper-laden finger into my nose and worked it deep into the nasal cavity. A painful burning sensation shot through my forehead. I ran the back of my hand across my nose and saw thick green discharge.

The cayenne was working! My congestion was clearing!

My friends were seconds away from Robo-Nose snorting them up forever. I charged at the evil smelling machine, blowing the contents of my snuffler directly into the nasally clone's nostrils like I was giving it nose-to-nose resuscitation.

I fell away, gasping for air. Robo-Nose's nostrils closed shut. It let out a deep choking sound, like it was fighting for breath. The Apneans who were guarding my friends rushed toward their wounded leader.

"Run!" I shouted. "This snorter's going to explode!"

We all dashed into the woods and watched the scene unfold. The booger blobs flying overhead ignored us and soared to help Robo-Nose.

"Listen," Vivian said. "The earthquake has stopped."

"She's right," TJ said. "I don't feel any more tremors."

"And the crack in the earth isn't getting any bigger," Mumps added.

Dr. Wackjöb opened his mouth to comment just as Robo-Nose began to suffocate. The alien ship's titanium seams split apart like an elephant trying to fit into a pair of pants made for a toddler.

Robo-Nose exploded in a violent shock wave. We all hit the ground as a shower of shrapnel fragments splintered off in every direction. A fireball scorched the area with red-hot flames.

"Keep your heads down," Dr. Wackjöb said.

"The blast wind is coming."

"What's a blast wind?" Jimmy asked.

Before Jimmy could get an explanation, a rush of air like a vacuum began sucking us toward the blast sight. The pull was so strong, we had to grab trees to keep the suction from drawing us back to the source of the explosion.

Then everything grew eerily silent.

The only sounds we heard were Robo-Nose's sizzling nose hairs.

The Apneans had disappeared, and the few remaining booger blobs were fleeing into the atmosphere toward outer space.

CHAPTER 25
WACKJÖB
ENTERPRISES

The Apneans had completely destroyed the Center for UFOs, Earthquakes, and Alien Abduction.

The steady hum of a helicopter's rotating wings buzzed in the distance.

"A helicopter is coming," I alerted everyone.

"That's a helicopter from the US Forest Service," Dr. Wackjöb said. "They probably saw the explosion from the top of Mt. Washington and are coming to investigate."

"Great!" TJ chirped. "We can tell them what happened out here. How we saved the world from an alien invasion!"

"Nobody's telling anybody anything," I told him. "Our operation is a secret. Remember?"

"But we deserve some recognition! We can be national heroes. They'll name high schools after us, stretches of highway, skyscrapers, airports. I can see it now: The TJ International Airport of Denmark, New Hampshire."

"McDonalds can name a new hamburger after me," Mumps said. "The McMumps Burger! Four all-beef patties, three slices of cheese, and lots of mustard!"

"That's about the grossest sounding burger ever," Vivian said and pretended to gag. "I'm glad I'm a vegetarian."

Dr. Wackjöb stood up and gazed at the ruins of his life's work. His face was haggard and old-looking. We had been through so much together; I felt bad for the guy. After all, his whole life had exploded in a wad of snot right up Robo-Nose's nostrils.

"TJ, the authorities will never believe you," Dr. Wackjöb said. "I have been trying to tell people for twenty years that alien beings are real and were planning an all-out assault on Earth. No one listened and they laughed me right out of Iceland."

"What will you do now?" Vivian asked.

Dr. Wackjöb shook his head in defeat. "My reputation has already been ruined and now my compound is completely destroyed. I have nowhere to go."

"You can stay in Denmark and be one of us," I said.

"Of course!" Vivian beamed. "You can be a new member of our team—Super Schnoz, the Not-Right Brothers, Vivian, and Dr. Wackjöb!"

"Great idea," Mumps said. "It's just like when the Human Torch became a member of the Fantastic Four."

"My dad owns an apartment building on Main Street," TJ added. "There are a couple of empty apartments. You can live in one of them."

A smile slowly spread across Dr. Wackjöb's wrinkly face. "You are very kind," he said softly. "I accept your offer as it appears I have no other choice."

148

"Besides Dr. Wackjöb joining our team, another good thing has come from all of this," Jimmy said.

"What's that?" I asked.

"Your snoring. We cured it. Now the people of Denmark can finally get a good night's sleep."

He was right. Without the Apneas shoving hoses up my nose every night, I was snore free. Now the townspeople wouldn't make my family and me move! I walked across the scorched battlefield and picked up the tub that held the sticky concoction Dr. Wackjöb and TJ had made. There was still a cupful sloshing around in the bottom.

"This potion you guys made worked like a charm," I said. "If it wasn't for this stuff, we'd all be speaking Apnean right now. That was the gooiest, stickiest stuff I've ever seen."

"I was just the helper," TJ said. "Dr. Wackjöb gets all the credit."

"Someone should market it as a product for glue," Vivian suggested. "You'd make a million."

Dr. Wackjöb's solemn face grew brighter. His

eyes opened wide in realization, like he'd just discovered the secret of the universe. He scooped the last few drops of his creation into a plastic cup. "Children, we need to get away from this place now," he said. "The US Forest Service and the State Police will be here any moment."

Vivian, the Not-Right Brothers, Dr. Wackjöb, and I walked down the path and headed back to town.

On the last day of summer vacation before school started back up, I slipped out of the house and hopped on my bike. My neighbors were getting ready for work, their faces fresh from a restful night's sleep. I pedaled into town as Main Street was just starting to liven up with the morning rush.

All but one coffee shop had closed its doors. Stores like the Soundproofing Emporium, the White Noise Outlet, and the Earthquake Emergency Bargain Bin had gone out of business too. But the storefronts were not empty. New businesses had set up shop, like Glue More, Forever Stick, Snore Be Gone Bazaar, and the Snore No More Shack.

When the earthquakes stopped, the North American Seismological Laboratory moved out of the old toothpick factory and back to California. The new occupant of the brick building was Wackjöb Enterprises—Makers of Gecko Glue® and Snore Cure Mist®.

A large sign outside of town proclaimed: Denmark, New Hampshire—the Glue and Anti-Snore Capital of the World.

After experimenting more with the sticky, snotty gunk, Dr. Wackjöb discovered that by boiling down the synthetic setae into a mist it transformed into a cure for snoring. He wasn't sure why, but after several clinical trials the facts were undisputable.

Dr. Aðalbjörn Wackjöb, native of Iceland and resident of Denmark, New Hampshire, had discovered a permanent cure for snoring.

I pedaled past Dr. Wackjöb's factory toward the outskirts of town. There was a rumor going around that a dead moose was lying on the side of a country road. I had been neglecting my scent dictionary as of late and was eager to add some new smells. A decaying, maggoty dead moose would be a perfect new addition.

I felt a slight sting on my nostril. I reached up and gently touched my nose. The wound on my honker from the nose hair-rocket was healing, but it still hurt sometimes.

From down the road of I heard a loud sucking sound. The noise sounded exactly the slurping of a booger blob's phlegm-powered engine! I ripped open my backpack, threw on my Super Schnoz cape and Mardi Gras mask, and searched the ground for fallen pinecones. The nearby woods were full of them, so I shoved a dozen or so up my nose and waited for the booger blob.

The snotty thing was coming up over the hill! The sickly slurping sound was unmistakable. Just as I was about to fire, I saw that it wasn't a booger blob after all. Just a rickety old pick-up truck with a bad muffler.

Relieved, I unloaded my nose of all the pinecones except for one. If a real booger blog appeared on the horizon, I wanted to be ready.

CHAPTER 1

STRANGE SCENT

"Schnoz, what's that weird smell?" Jimmy asked me one day while TJ, Mumps, Vivian, and I were cruising on our bikes down Main Street.

I flared my nostrils and inhaled the luscious, intoxicating scent. My nose hairs tingled with joy. My olfactory bulbs throbbed with delight. The wonderful smell had been wafting in the crisp autumn air of Denmark, New Hampshire, for weeks and my nose could barely contain its excitement.

"That smell isn't weird," I answered. "It's *Strange*, as in Jean Paul Puanteur's *Strange*."

"Huh?" TJ grunted.

"*Strange* is the name of an extremely popular unisex perfume." Vivian said, steering her bike toward Dr. Wackjöb's Gecko Glue® and Snore Cure Mist® factory. "Every teenager and adult in town wears it."

"What's unisex mean?" Jimmy asked.

I hit the brakes and my bike skidded to a stop. "It means the perfume is suitable for both sexes, male and female.

TJ laughed. "Perfume's for girls."

"Don't tell that to my dad," Mumps said. "He's been spraying himself with Strange every morning for a month."

"My mom loves it, too," Vivian added. "She's goes through a bottle every two weeks."

"Jean Paul Puanteur is the greatest perfumer in the world!" I proclaimed. "He's the Mozart of odor, the Picasso of aroma!"

"Schnoz, let me give you a piece of advice," Jimmy razzed. "Don't let the other guys in school know you like perfume. It could be seriously bad for your honker health."

Before I could respond, one of Dr. Wackjöb's

delivery trucks whizzed past us. His Gecko Glue® and Snore Cure Mist® products were selling like hotcakes around the world. In fact, they were so successful that Filthy Rich Review magazine had featured the company on the cover of its October issue. But the best thing about the business was that it employed hundreds of local people. My mom even got a job there as a quality control supervisor.

"I don't care what anyone thinks," I said to Jimmy after the truck had turned the corner. "I'm not just a one-sniff pony who only likes the smells of dog poop, armpits, and rotting road kill. I'm a connoisseur of the sweeter scents in life too, you know."

"The art of mixing herb oil, spices, and tree resins to make different fragrances goes all the way back to ancient Babylon," Vivian said. "Perfuming is as old as civilization itself."

TJ rolled his eyes. "Ancient or not, I still say perfume is for girls."

"Stop being a sexist!" Vivian yelled and then held up her fists. "Do you want a bop on the chin?"

"I'm not six!" TJ fired back. "I turned eleven two months ago."

"I said you were a *sexist*, dork butt. A person who stereotypes people based on their gender."

"She's right, TJ," I said. "Apologize. Vivian's smarter and tougher than all of you Not-Right Brothers put together."

TJ kicked a rock. "I'm sorry, but I didn't mean anything by it. I just assumed only girls wore perfume, that's all."

"Well, now you know different," Vivian said. "Let's hurry up and get to Dr. Wackjöb's office. I'm starving."

Every Wednesday was early release day from school so the teachers could have meetings. We got out at noon and, weather permitting, always rode our bikes to Dr. Wackjöb's office for lunch. As we rode down the street toward the factory, I inhaled the overpowering smell of *Strange* that drifted through the Denmark air.

Distinguishing between the perfume's different ingredients proved difficult at first, but soon my powerful olfactory receptors downloaded the parts directly into my mental scent dictionary. The perfume's base was ethyl alcohol and distilled water. Next, I sniffed a tantalizing blend of essential oils like lavender, jasmine, sandalwood, and bergamot. I could tell the perfume was of the highest quality because all the ingredients were natural, not one synthetic fragrance in the mix.

The security guard at Dr. Wackjöb's opened the factory gates and we rolled into the parking lot. I leaned my bike on the rack, took one stop toward the office door, and that's when I sensed another extremely subtle, barely detectable ingredient in the *Strange* concoction. The odor stopped me in my tracks. My nose lifted into the air, huffing like a crazed bloodhound at the scent particles floating on the wind.

"What's wrong, Schnoz?" Vivian asked. "You look like you just smelled a ghost."

"I smell something, all right," I said, my heart thumping. "And I have no idea what it is."

"But you know practically every smell on earth," Mumps said.

I scanned my mental scent dictionary front to back, starting with the pungent odor of a crushed ant to the cheesy aroma of baked ziti. There was nothing, not one tiny whiff of the *Strange* scent.

CHAPTER 2

FRENCH JASMINE

Dr. Wackjöb was chatting on the phone when his secretary escorted us into his office. The overwhelming stench of fresh Hákarl blasted up my nostrils. I loved the smell of fermented, urine-soaked shark meat, but the Icelandic delicacy made Vivian and the Not-Right Brothers nearly gag.

Jimmy pulled his t-shirt up over his nose. "Why does Dr. Wackjöb have to eat that disgusting Hákarl every single day for lunch?"

"I don't like the smell, either," Vivian said. "But we have to give the guy a break. The doctor was a laughing stock in his native Iceland and had to flee. Hákarl reminds him of home."

"Hákarl reminds me of an unflushed toilet," Mumps said with a grimace.

"So nice to hear from you, Pierre, and I hope to speak with you soon." Dr. Wackjöb said and then hung up the phone. He pointed to three large pizza boxes sitting on a conference table. "One is plain, one is pepperoni, and the other is black olives and mushrooms. Please, help yourselves."

Vivian, the Not-Brothers, and I tore into the pizzas like starving rescue dogs. Dr. Wackjöb tied a bib around his neck and popped slices of Hákarl into his mouth. He chewed very slowly, savoring each and every shark pee–flavored bite.

While the gang munched away, my nose drifted off to the mysterious smell locked inside *Strange*. The fragrance resembled vanilla, but the unknown aroma was way more earthy, funky, and bold than any variety I had ever come across during my scent gathering expeditions. Only a master like Jean Paul Puanteur could confuse my world-class sniffer like this!

Most kids my age have posters of actors, musicians, and athletes hanging on their bedroom walls. As for me, I have only a small, 8x10-framed picture of Jean Paul Puanteur. I had clipped the photo from a *National Geographic* magazine article about the art and science of making perfume. He is standing in a field of extremely rare and expensive French jasmine, a brilliant orange sun high in the sky. The man is a scent artist of the highest order.

A set of greasy fingers snapped in front of my face.

"Earth to Schnoz," Vivian said, ripping me out of my French jasmine daze. "You're staring blankly into space. What are you thinking about?"

"*Strange*," I said.

TJ fanned the air in front of his face. "I wish I had a bottle of *Strange* right now. I'd spray it around the room to get rid of the Hákarl stink!"

Dr. Wackjob laughed. "Iceland's secret shark recipe goes all the way back to the time of Vikings. What is this *Strange* you speak of?"

"*Strange* is a ridiculously popular perfume," Mumps answered. "Everybody's wearing the stuff."

"I'm a huge fan of the perfuming arts," I said. "But there's one ingredient in *Strange* that my snuffer can't sniff out."

Dr. Wackjöb raised his white, bushy eyebrows. "You, the one and only Super Schnoz, cannot recognize a scent? I don't believe it. Your nose is to smells like Einstein's brain is to physics."

"Well, this is one odor equation I have yet to crack."

"I don't know anything about the perfume business," Dr. Wackjöb continued. "But just like my company has a secret ingredient—synthetic setae developed from the sticky pads on a gecko's feet—I would assume perfumers use secret ingredients as well."

I shrugged. "You're probably right, but if I don't figure out that smell and add it to my scent dictionary I'm going to blow a booger!"

"Perhaps I should call back Pierre and ask him."

"Who's Pierre?" Vivian asked.

"He's the gentleman I was talking to on the phone as you arrived for lunch. He's a Frenchman, an old friend of mine from when

I studied geology for a year at the *University Lille Nord de France*. I hadn't spoken with him in thirty years. He phoned me out of blue after reading about my successful business in *Filthy Rich Review* magazine."

"Why would this Pierre person know about secret ingredients found in perfume?" I asked.

"Gríðarstór Nef, my old friend's full name is Pierre du Voleur, owner of the Français Scent Company, makers of fine perfumes and fragrances."

I sat up in my seat, nose hairs quivering with excitement. "Can you ask him about the mystery ingredient in *Strange?*"

"That won't do any good," Vivian said.

"Why?"

"*Strange* is made by Jean Paul Puanteur, a completely different company. Coke would never give up its secret soda formula to Pepsi. Why would two rival perfume companies share ingredients?"

"She's right, Schnoz," Jimmy said. "If you want to figure out that smell, you'll have to huff it out for yourself."

The scent receptors inside my honker deflated a little. Now I knew how Peter Parker felt when he had to battle Venom in the *Amazing Spider Man #6*. The task would be daunting, but I had never met a smell my nose couldn't defeat, and *Strange* was not going to be the first.